Property of the Bad Boy

Vanessa Waltz

ISBN: 1515261417
ISBN-13: 978-1515261414

DEDICATION

Dedicated to my friend, Chuck. You're the best!

CONTENTS

ACKNOWLEDGMENTS

Thanks to Kevin McGrath for cover design and Faith Van Horne for editing.

JACK

Music pounds from the floor-to-wall speakers, radiating outward. The waves shake into my leg, traveling upward to bury somewhere in my chest. The bass plays my rib cage like a drum, and I lift the cool glass to my lips—I don't remember what the fuck I'm drinking—and I tilt my head back. A vague burning sensation fills my mouth as multicolored lights bleed into each other.

Jesus, I'm wasted.

I'm wasted a lot lately.

A hand pounds my shoulder really fucking hard, and I turn around, glass in hand. The whole world turns with me in swirls of color. I'm ready to smash the drink in his face, but it's only François. He gives me a look that boils my blood. That upturned nose and those haughty eyes condemn me.

Go ahead and judge me, you fuck.

Like anyone in my position would be sober.

His mouth moves, and it takes a few seconds to work out what he's saying. "Are you ready to go?"

"Am I balls deep in some chick right now?"

He rolls his eyes.

"I came here to get laid, and I'm not leaving until that happens."

We went out tonight celebrating my last night of freedom, but so far it's a fucking letdown. Johnny's axe hangs over my neck, and I keep thinking about that instead of scoring easy pussy.

"Keeping the boss waiting isn't smart, Jack."

Fuck the boss.

François's jovial face falls ever so slightly as heat rises to my skin. It's almost as if I said it out loud. Maybe I would say it if I had a death wish, but I don't want to think about that piece of shit right now. My head turns, swimming in colors and perfume and the hundreds of bodies, smashed together. Ignoring him, I slide into the thick of the dance floor. I came here for pussy. One last wild night.

Used to be that I had wild nights every fucking night. A new day, a new girl. Easy and simple is how I like it, and getting a hot piece of ass to follow me to bed was never hard. A roll of cash and a few soft words on their ears would usually do the trick, but some girls don't go for that. Some girls want me to whisper something dirty in their ears. They want the filth. They want me to talk about making them come with my tongue. I'll tell them how big my dick is. None of them believe me, and then it's easy to persuade them to go somewhere so that I can show them privately. Some of them are wild for action. They want excitement in their lives. Then all I have to do is show the gun hanging at my hip and tell them that I work "in construction," and they're mine for the evening.

There are beautiful girls everywhere, wearing shorts with tattered strings that brush over the swell of their nicely tanned asses, just begging for a squeeze. A tall blonde pushes her hair back shyly and smiles at me, but she's not really my type. Nice tits though. I keep squeezing my way through, but it's impossible to be heard, and I'm not about to throw a girl over my shoulder and walk out.

This isn't working. There are too many lights and sounds. Frankly

I'm in danger of falling on my ass, and heat presses in on me from all sides. I feel like I'm in a straitjacket. By the time I make my way back to the bar, François is gone. He fucked off somewhere. Good.

The bartender looks up as I arrive, making me a drink before I can even sit down. If I didn't know any better, I'd think she was trying to take advantage of me. She knows who I am—the people I'm connected to. That alone keeps the drinks flowing all night.

I sit down on the small black stool and eye the poured drink ruefully. There's no fucking *way* I can have another one, not when I don't even feel like I have limbs anymore.

"Hey."

A timid, feminine voice filters through the bullshit blasting on the speakers, and I turn my head to the left.

Wow.

It's like a mirage. A stunning girl sits on the stool next to mine. It takes a while for me to get the details of her into focus, like the white spaghetti-strap tank top she's wearing, and the little red flowers decorating it. Her tits are perky and I have to resist the urge to look at her cleavage. She makes my cock throb. I look down her thin waist to the jeans sticking to her ass like skin and then back to her face. Long, highlighted blonde hair brushes her slight, feminine shoulders. She has a vulnerable look about her that is completely at odds with her amazing body. Her eyes are wide and blue, and there's a small dusting of freckles on her nose and cheeks. A girl like her should be brimming with confidence, but instead she plays with her glass, her rose-painted fingernails running up the sides incessantly. It's my job to notice people's weaknesses. To assess and exploit. It's my bread and butter, so to speak. This girl screams "inexperienced," and my dick jumps at the thought of being the one to break her—to shove my cock inside her tight pussy and watch her shatter as I take her wide-eyed innocence.

"Hey, sexy." Goddamn it, I'm still drunk as hell.

Thankfully she just smiles at me, laughter all over her face. "You're not so bad yourself."

Hello.

"Oh, that's one thing I already know."

She laughs, a bell-like sound. "Do you want to have a drink with me?"

You can do anything you want to me, baby.

I study her jittering ankle. She's nervous. That's cute. A smile spreads across my face, and I beckon to her with a finger. "Come here."

Pink rises in her cheeks as she hesitantly slides off the stool and takes a few steps toward me. I grab her wrist and yank her forward so that her body stumbles and then I pull her over my lap. She wraps her arms around my neck with a surprised gasp.

"I'd rather have a taste of you."

For a moment she just eye-fucks me as the tiny freckles dotting her nose burn. My hands snake around her waist and I feel the heat of her burning through the thin fabric of her camisole.

"That's a pretty good line."

"Give me a fucking kiss."

I love feeling the weight of her on my lap. Her hair tickles my skin as she leans forward, her pale lips hovering over my face. Sweetness flows over my tongue as I catch her bottom lip, crushing my mouth against hers. A spicy, ginger smell wafts from her hair, which is as smooth as silk. There's nothing like having a gorgeous woman on your lap. Nothing like having a gorgeous *naked* woman on your lap, playing with your clothes and ready to do your bidding. Fuck, my slacks tighten just thinking about it. I want to feel her smooth skin gliding in my hands, and I want her to feel my rock-hard cock riding against her bare ass. Thank God I don't get whiskey dick.

She pulls away from me before I can stick my tongue down her throat. I watch how she sucks in breath through those small pink lips that I'd love to see wrapped around my cock. She's close enough to kiss again. Close enough to do anything I want, which is to drag my tongue down her neck to her milky cleavage.

Look at her tits. Do it.

But I force myself to hold her gaze. My heart does a small flip when her lips pull away, revealing a row of white, even teeth. Damn, she has a beautiful smile.

"You're a very good kisser."

Blood pounds in my head, my vision still swimming with booze. "There are a lot of other things I'm good at. Want me to show you?"

A laughing, sweet smile fills her face, as if she can't believe what she's hearing. "Let's have a drink."

Disappointment settles in my guts and then I realize that she just wants to talk bullshit for a while so that she feels less bad about her one-night stand.

"I can't have another drink. Look at me."

"You don't look very drunk."

"Trust me, *I am.*"

But not drunk enough to not see how the skin on top of her breast jumps with her pulse. Or feel the blood pounding through my cock. *Elle est belle en tabarnak*. I only have half an hour before I have to leave, and I have to fuck this girl. For fuck's sake, she made the first move. This should be easy.

"But I can still give you the best night of your fucking life."

"What do you mean by that?"

"I'll make your toes curl, baby."

"Uh-huh."

"I'll fill you up until you scream. You'll never feel so sore and good after a night with my cock."

A few seconds of stunned silence follow my words and then I turn my head to kiss that throbbing vein in her neck. Her nails dig into me ever so slightly.

Good. I have her.

She clears her throat. "What makes you think you can even use that cock in your condition?"

My blood churns at the salty tone in her voice. Fuck, I love girls with attitude. "Babe, I've fucked women when I was much more wasted than this."

"Yeah?" Her chest flushes with red. "And how many of them want a second time with you?"

A smile hitches on my face. "All of them."

She shakes her head, not believing me.

I slip my phone out of my slacks, still very conscious of her ass sitting on my lap, right over my cock. I show her my text messages, a dozen or so unread ones with random numbers. I pick one at random:

OMG that was so hot last night let's get together again r u free Friday?

She snorts with laughter and then she goes back, selecting another one:

I will literally suck your dick off if we go out again. I do anal.

This time she throws her head back and laughs, the phone shaking in her hand. It's a beautiful sound that makes a hot drop of pleasure run down my throat. I take the phone from her, chuckling.

"See?"

"Why do you get their numbers if you never call them back?"

I shrug as a shard of unpleasantness suddenly bursts the bubble of my happiness. The truth is just far too depressing.

"I don't know."

She smiles at me, and I don't think I'll ever forget that smile. My heart bumps a little when she slides her hands around my neck.

"You're here alone, aren't you?"

She nods as a deep blush fills her face. "Yeah."

Perfect.

My mouth hovers over her ear. I brush back her hair with a finger and her shoulders shiver.

"Do you want to go somewhere to talk—in private?"

I figure that's more polite than, *I want to fuck you.*

Her head turns, her lips inches from mine. I'm startled by the warmth gripping my insides when an uncertain smile pricks her face. "I don't know."

"Yes, you do."

She jerks her head to the side. "I *don't.*"

"Why offer to buy me a drink, then?"

Her heated gaze falls back over me, strong but unsure. "'Cause I—" She breaks off with a chuckle of bitter laughter. "Never mind. I should go."

Her body slides from my lap, but I catch her before she can fall, wrapping both arms tightly around her small waist. She turns to me with a scandalized look.

"*Hey!*"

My chest rumbles with a small laugh. "I'm not letting your sweet ass out of my sight until I get what I want from you." My mouth hovers right over hers. "Thirty minutes. Alone."

"Thirty minutes? What— Is that some kind of joke?"

Her eyebrows arch high right before I spread my palm on her back and drag my fingernails down.

"If I'm not the best fucking lay you've ever had after thirty minutes, I don't deserve to call myself a man."

Fingers clench the back of my head.

"Okay."

Awesome.

I stand up from my stool and deposit her to the floor gently, holding out my hand for her to grab. She slides a smooth hand in mine and then I curl my arm around her waist, feeling her rapid breaths as her cheeks blaze. I leave a tip for the bartender and climb the stairs to the VIP rooms, which I hope are deserted. A quick glance through the glass doors tells me no.

Fuck.

I open the door to a room filled with soft purple leather couches, the black lights emitting an annoying dark haze over the whole room. A loud group sits in one of the couches, but there's no way I'm fucking this girl with a crowd of people listening in, so I make a beeline for them.

My eyes meet the surly gaze of some backwards-baseball-cap-wearing douchebag.

"Johnny Cravotta needs the room emptied. *Get out.*"

"Shit—he's here?"

"That's none of your concern."

As a matter of fact he's not, but it's not like Douchebag will try to challenge a wise guy. They exchange worried looks and rise from the couch, filing out one by one as the door finally shuts us into silence.

The girl's arm trembles at my side and I take it, leading her to an empty couch. She sits down like a small bird and I sink into the leather beside her, curling an arm over her shoulders. Her curves press into my side as she twists her body, my blood pounding where she daintily touches my leg. Heat spreads across her pulsing chest. The red blush fills her skin like a fever. I slip my fingers under her white spaghetti strap and caress her shoulder. I have half a mind to pull it down. She's not wearing anything else underneath— *Holy fuck*; I'm hard as a rock.

Her tremulous voice breathes out again. "Do you have a girlfriend? Wife?"

Not yet.

"No."

It's fun watching her squirm. Desire parts her lips as I continue my slow massage of her shoulder. Her eyes keep lingering on my face—my lips. Blonde hair shifts, obscuring her face from view.

"I—uh—*fuck*," she laughs into her hands. "I'm so embarrassed."

My other hand touches her chin, and she turns back toward me. Warm breath mists over my mouth and for a moment I can't hear anything but the roaring sound of my blood.

"You shouldn't be shy."

"Why's that?"

"Because a girl like you gets whatever she wants. All you have to do is ask."

"I just—"

I hear her sharp intake of breath just before I close in the few inches between us. My lips touch hers as the hand playing with her shoulder snakes into a tangle of her hair. Heat smolders between us as she kisses me back, hesitant at first and then more forceful. She shoves the jacket from my shoulders and finds the space under my neck to touch my bare skin. Then I'm on fire—my hand falls down her shoulder to grab one of her tits. The fabric is so fucking thin that I can feel the stiff peak of her nipple. My thumb caresses the hard nub and a high, desperate sound leaves her mouth to enter mine.

Jesus Christ.

I want this fucking girl. I want her tits in my mouth and her pussy swallowing my cock, but I only have a half hour before I really have to leave.

Pick up the fucking pace, Jack.

She pulls back and I inwardly groan as she gives a little shake of her head.

"What's wrong, sweetheart?"

"I'm supposed to be somewhere."

"Me too." My hand reaches down her back, grabbing the edge of the camisole and dragging it up, over her skin. Her eyes widen like saucers as I lift it over her creamy white globes and all the way up. I fling the camisole away and cover her tits with my hands. Fucking gorgeous tits. "I'll fuck you really nice and fast—that's what you want, isn't it?"

I'm distracted by the feeling of them in my hands, and a low growl issues from my throat when she nods.

"What's your name?"

Her heartbeat slams into my hand and I just want to rip the rest of her clothes off, but she drags her fingers up and down the back of my neck.

A smile staggers across my face. "It's Jack."

"I'm Beatrice."

"Hello, Beatrice." My mouth fastens over her nipple and she gasps as I take the other one between my thumb and forefinger, pinching hard as I drag my tongue over her skin and suck. She clutches my neck and digs her fingers, letting out a loud moan that surprises me.

I might as well taste all of her. I did promise to be the best lay she ever had.

"Stand up, sweetheart. Do it now."

My teeth bite into her wonderful, jiggling tits before I smack her ass. I see the red mark blazing on her white skin as she pulls away to stand up in front of me shyly. Her lips are plump and wet, and the way her hair looks slightly mussed up makes me want to bend her over the coffee table. She sucks in her bottom lip and bites it. My cock throbs, growing along my leg like a steel pipe.

"Take off your clothes. All of them."

I watch as my command runs through her body. She hesitates, looking over her shoulder at the glass windows.

"Do as I say."

Her head snaps back as she sucks in a deep breath, hooking her thumbs in the waistband of her jeans and pulling them down with agonizing slowness. They drag over her bony hips, revealing a shaved pussy gleaming with wetness. My mouth waters to see the rest of her creamy thighs and calves. I follow her hands all the way down until her feet step out of her jeans.

"Get that beautiful pussy in my face."

A thrill hits my chest as she steps forward, following my every command. Damn, she likes taking orders, doesn't she? It's hot. My eyes are on the sheen of wetness sticking to her inner thighs. My cock strains against my slacks as she stands on the couch uncertainly. My hand slides up the back of her thigh, right up to her tight ass. I fondle her perfect bubble and then I strike her hard. Her muscles twitch and she lets out a sharp gasp.

"*Closer.*"

"But I've never—"

My hands circle her thighs as she stands up on the couch, bringing me face-to-face with her pussy, which is the exact same shade of pink as her blush. I don't give a fuck that we're exposed to the entire club—I can't waste another second without my tongue inside her. My lips touch her clit and my tongue slides against her sweetness.

"*Oh my God!*"

She curls her fingers in my hair and yanks hard enough to make me grunt.

I guess she likes it.

I reach back with my tongue all the way and slide along her slippery folds, feeling her rock against my mouth as her body gives in to pleasure. Her pussy drips and I drink her in, enjoying the mild taste as her muscles clench around my tongue. Then I grind against her, shoving myself deep inside her cunt as I massage her soaking clit with my thumb. I feel my briefs getting wet with the pre-cum slipping out of my cock, and I so badly want to rip my pants off and yank her down over me. I kiss her, circling her nub as my fingers slip inside her. Goddamn, she's so wet for me.

I hammer her cunt with my two fingers, sucking her reddened flesh as she grips my hair and screams something in my ear.

"Kiss me!"

Shit.

I pull her hips down so that she falls to my lap. Soft, round tits smash against my chest as she throws her arms around me and crushes her mouth to mine. My body falls backward and I just manage to catch myself with an arm thrown behind myself. Her voice is raw, panting as she kisses me, sweeping inside my mouth to taste herself. Feeling her wild tongue inside me makes me wonder what it'd feel like to have her swallow my cock, but we're pressed on time. Fucking *hell.*

Her nails drag over my skin, scratching me as she rips off my dress shirt. Scattering buttons hit the marble floor. I sit up as she yanks the shirt from my body, my heart pounding hard, driving alcohol from my head.

Heat simmers just below the surface of where she touches me. She runs her fingers over my muscles, her rosebud mouth flushed from kissing me. I grab the back of her head and twist her long hair into a rope, kissing her neck. She gasps.

"Lie down and spread your legs."

Then my hand slips from her neck and my heart pounds against my skin as she looks up at me, her eyes wide. They're so blue. She obeys me, her tits spreading over her chest as she lies down. I just want to throttle through and fuck her until the whole club can hear her screams, but the vulnerability in her eyes stops me. I follow her gaze below my belt, to my livid erection pressing absurdly against my slacks. She flinches as I undo my belt and fling it aside. Then I walk right to her head and pull down my slacks and briefs. Veins throb along my cock and a glistening bead of pre-cum hangs precariously as my dick springs free from my pants. I fist the base of it and watch her lick her lips.

"You like it, sweetheart? Want to touch it?"

A grin tightens my face as she reaches up and grabs me with both hands, moving up and down as if she's never touched a cock before. She cups my balls with one, the other held firmly at the base. My cock jumps in her hands.

"You're so big."

"I've primed your pussy so that I could fuck you with every inch."

I reach down and grab one of her tits as she plays with me, and then she looks at me with an uncertain gleam, her lips inches from my cock.

"Can I?"

She leans forward before I can respond, licking the pebble of pre-cum from my head. I squeeze her tits hard as she starts forward again, wrapping her lips around my head. A deep sigh leaves my throat as her tongue slides underneath, all the sensitive nerves on fire from her mouth. Now she's sucking my cock, her beautiful, innocent eyes looking at me shyly, as if for approval. It's fucking hot.

"Don't be shy, take it all the way."

Using my hand, I apply pressure to the back of her head and watch my cock slowly disappear in her throat. She pulls back to breathe, my dick greased with her saliva, and then she tries again.

"I want your nose to touch right here."

I point to the skin right above my groin.

Shit, I love blowjobs. Sloppy, wet, noisy blowjobs, and this girl seems to be the queen of them. She grabs the base of my dick hard and runs her tongue along my shaft, gagging herself, and my muscles flex. It's so hard not to just grab her head and fuck her throat, especially when she reaches around to grab my ass, pushing my cock deeper inside. My cock touches the back of her mouth, and then her nose touches my body. Good God, any more and I'll come inside her.

"Good girl," I say in a heavy voice, feeling as though I'm drunk again. "Very, very good girl."

I love the view. Gorgeous, naked girl, sucking my cock. She moves on all fours and grabs my hips, and I can't stop admiring her. The way her back dips, the delicate curve of her spine leading to her perfect ass, still pink with the imprint of my hand.

"Stop."

My cock throbs against her lips as she gives me a questioning look, and I bend over as her creamy neck arches with my hand gently pulling the back of her head. Then I seal my kiss against her lips, grabbing her one of her tits with a rough hand, feeling their orbicular shape, the way they bounce in my hands. Fuck, I can't believe how hard I am. I taste myself inside her mouth, my tongue playing with hers. My hand slips lower, away from her chest to her other curves. What a nice ass. So tight I could probably bounce a penny off her. Then I sweep around her hip to that pussy that's already creaming for me.

Her head lolls on my arm when my two fingers slide inside her tight walls, her eyes lit in an expression of ecstasy. I slide them in torturously slow, watching how she twists and how her legs move and how she bites her lip and moans anyway. She's a sexy sight. I keep finger-fucking her, increasing the pace as her pussy gets soaking wet—the sounds unnaturally loud. Perhaps it's because I can only see and hear her, and my dick feels like it's going to fall off soon if I don't hammer that perfectly primed cunt.

But I want to get her as close to the edge as possible. I pride myself on my abilities, on leaving every girl satisfied. I don't want this girl satisfied—I want her floating on cloud nine; I want her to sing ballads about my cock.

She grasps my neck with her dainty fingers and moans into my mouth like a slut. Blood pounds in my head like a hammer. I've never been so worked up in my goddamn life. It's the sounds she makes.

"Jack, please."

I slide my fingers out of her, my cock jumping when I hold them to my face and suck every drop of her.

"You taste so fucking good."

Red flames lick her cheeks.

"I think I'm going to take turns fucking you and jamming my tongue as far as I can inside that sweet pussy. How does that sound?"

She kisses me. No, she *attacks* me with her arms winding around my neck and her tongue down my throat. Her fingernails rake the back of my neck, and it's fucking hot, but I push her back gently so that her heaving body lies on the couch.

Get the fucking condom.

I nearly rip the thing in half as I fish it out of my pants and roll it on my iron-stiff cock. She's just the perfect sight. Nothing better than a wet and willing woman, legs already open for you.

She wraps her legs around me and I guide the head between her folds, feeling that first bit of resistance. I slowly sink into her and she lets out a high gasp. I look at her, and her face is contorted.

What the hell?

"What's the matter?"

She pulls me down and I'm sure the vein on my forehead is ready to blow. I'm halfway inside this girl and I want to *fuck* the shit out of her. Her eyes are wide and her chest pulses hard, but she clings to my neck. I slide another inch inside, feeling how tight her walls are. I plant a kiss on her damp neck.

"You need to relax."

"I—it's been a while."

Oh, fucking great.

"Do you want me to stop?"

Please, God, say no.

"No. *Please.*"

I thrust again, hearing her breath hitch in her chest. I just love seeing her reaction to my huge cock.

"It's so fucking big."

"I told you I was going to bury every inch inside you."

I give her a moment to adjust and then I thrust a little harder. Her muscles loosen around me and she squeezes my head, raking her nails up and down my back.

She clenches around me as I drive into her harder. Gradually I feel her let go. She digs her nails into my neck, raking them down until she anchors over my ass.

"Oh my God, it feels so amazing."

"I told you."

I wait until her breaths start to quicken. Until every thrust rends a moan from her throat. Until I feel like I'm going to explode. Then I pull out, and her flushed face narrows at me. "What are you doing?"

I shift my body so that her legs curl over my back and shove my face to her steaming cunt. It's swollen with arousal. As soon as my lips touch her she clenches her thighs around my face.

"Jesus!"

I breathe into her pussy, sliding my tongue over the bud that makes her scream. My fingers spread her open and my tongue slips inside. Her pussy keeps clenching over my tongue as I drive it in as far as I can, closing my mouth over it to drink her. I stroke her thighs, even reach to touch her stomach. Her muscles twitch under my fingers and then she bends, sitting upright. She grabs my hair.

I love the ferocity on her face. She shudders when I give her a clit a kiss.

"Lie down, sweetheart. I'm not done."

She pulls on the roots of my hair. "But I want you *now*."

It takes everything inside me not to climb back over her and go to town. "I'm going to spank you if I have to ask you again."

Then her fingers loosen from my hair and I stick out my tongue. I slide up and down, waiting for her to gasp or moan, the sound hitting my cock. Jesus Christ, I have to shove my dick inside that wet pussy. I suck her hard, just flicking my tongue against her sensitive bud. She arches her back and grasps her hair.

"Please!"

Jesus fuck, I can't take it anymore.

I get back on the couch, shoving myself between her as I come face-to-face with her, guiding my cock through her wetness. The urgency builds inside me like a pulsing ache, and I grab her tiny waist. I watch her eyes go wide when I shove my cock inside her, again and again. She claws my ass, and she's so wet that the sound of my balls slapping her pussy echoes loudly in the room. The sounds she makes—the howling, the begging—fuck, it's hot. Then I reach down and I pinch her clit just as I feel my stomach seize with a violent tremor.

"Fuck!"

I cover her mouth with mine as the pressure building up in my cock finally explodes. My hips thrust into her as I moan loud enough to surprise myself. She buries her fingers in my hair, breathing hard against my lips. I watch those blue eyes break as she succumbs to the orgasm shaking through her body. She clings to my neck and kisses me as aftershocks of my orgasm rip through me, thrusting my hips.

Goddamn, I came really hard.

I prop myself on my elbows and I wipe away a strand of hair sticking to her forehead. Her face breaks into a wide smile.

"That was amazing."

"I told you, didn't I?"

Her cheeks burn a dark fuchsia, and I wonder why I'm not already on my way, picking my clothes off the floor and making some excuse why I can't stay. I'm still here, balls deep inside her. Something freezes me in place. Maybe it's the way she's still begging me with those eyes.

"What's that look?"

Her eyes are so fucking blue.

"I thought you'd be different."

I make a noise through my nose.

"I thought you'd be an asshole."

I trace her plump bottom lip. An aftershock of my orgasm shakes through my body and I feel like I'm drunk on the smell of her hair. It takes me a while to respond. "Because?"

"You're a wise guy."

My stomach tightens. How did she find out?

You practically threatened that jock by dropping Johnny's name.

"Yeah, well, I'm not an asshole to women, but everyone else is shit out of luck."

The corners of her eyes wrinkle with a smile. "Tough guy, huh?"

My elbows sink into the couch cushions as I nuzzle her neck. When I plant a kiss on her throat, she utters a small gasp and I smile against her skin.

"You think you've got me pinned down?"

I pull back far enough so that her nose touches mine. Her shoulders lift in a shrug and she glances away shyly.

"Maybe."

"What about you?" A smile staggers across my face. "Let me guess: sheltered girl who had to sneak out so that she could get some dick."

"Close enough."

I knew it.

A tinge of regret hits me because no matter how hot the sex was, I won't see her again. I can't. I'm already dreading the moment I'll have to see the puzzled disappointment in her eyes.

She watches me, mouth half-open as if she wants to say something, and then the drowsy happiness fades from her eyes. Beatrice rolls on her side and reaches for her shirt. I pull out of her, unsticking my body from hers. Avoiding my gaze, she stands and picks up her clothes. I grab my slacks and stare at her, thrown by her behavior.

You should be glad you don't have to give her some excuse.

Beatrice stands awkwardly, watching me dress. An odd expression hangs on her face. Then I button my shirt, smirking at the destroyed threads of one of the buttons.

"All right. I have to go—"

"I—I want—"

She opens her mouth with an air of determination, but I take her face in my hands gently.

"If I could see you again, I would. Sorry, hon."

I kiss her stunned cheek and turn around before she can plead with me. Regret settles in my guts like lead. She was an incredibly hot lay, and maybe I would've called her. Fuck, you don't forget a girl who gives head like that.

"I'll see you soon, Jack Gallo."

A smile hitches on my face and my hand is on the doorknob before I realize I never gave that girl my last name.

* * *

How did she know my last name?

It bugs me the whole night, and I can't figure it out.

Do I know her?

I think I'd remember a girl like that. I keep slipping into earlier tonight, when I was banging the shit out of that smoking-hot girl—Beatrice. Definitely the best lay I've had in months.

Fucking focus.

I push thoughts of that girl out of my head.

The hospital is dark after midnight. They dim the hallways slightly and the rooms are blackened, and it's quiet except for an oppressive, electrical hum that puts me on edge. All these fucking computers and equipment. I want to take a bat to them.

I walk into the ICU, swiping the stolen badge over the wall, which unlocks the double doors. I stroll in and veer to the left, avoiding the nurse's station. My footsteps don't make much noise on the polished floor. Years of being a predator on the streets taught me how to keep quiet. I never thought I'd use it for this. Then I pass the room where he died and a vicious surge of energy hits my chest.

They're fucking animals. All of them.

A body hits my chest as I round the corner. He bounces off me and his clipboard goes flying, and I bend over quickly to pick it up.

Fuck.

"Sorry."

I hand over the clipboard and he rips it from me. I peer at his badge. Nathan Ross. The very same Nathan Ross I'm trying to find. Frustration bleeds into hot rage as my fists tighten at my sides.

"It's fine," he says in an irritated tone. "Can I help you?"

Yeah, you can help me. You piece of shit.

He looks young—probably the same age as me—but he looks like shit. There are cuts on his face where the retard shaves himself, and his haircut is uneven. Dark circles under his eyes indicate sleepless nights.

"No. Have a nice day."

I force myself to turn on the spot and walk away from him as every inch of me seethes. Won't have to wait that long.

I don't actually remember walking back to the parking garage. My eyes blink under the cover of the darkness, hands shaking. There's no fear, just searing-hot madness. A whistle cuts through the garage and I hide behind the concrete wall next to Nathan's car. His footsteps echo loudly and I make sure to hide under plain sight of the camera.

Another surge of hatred burns my insides. Whistling. *How the fuck can you whistle?*

A man dressed in blue scrubs walks beside me. I lunge at him like a snake, immobilizing him in seconds and smothering his mouth with my hand. He struggles violently, and my arm slides over his throat. I squeeze the vein throbbing on the side of his neck and wait until his body goes limp. I let him collapse to the floor, his head smacking against the concrete.

There's no point in killing him now. Then I fish in his pants for the keys to his car and I pop open the trunk. His body makes a dull sound as I throw him in there.

The drive doesn't soothe my nerves. I can hear him fucking around in the back, but it doesn't matter. Nothing matters. I expect him to pass out from the heat, but even that would be too good for that rat bastard. A horrifying image of my brother immobilized on the hospital bed flashes through my head, but I shove it away. Can't think of that now.

The car bounces as I drive through the uneven dirt road to the junkyard. His screams rebound inside the small trunk, and finally I park his car between two mounds of crushed metal and cut the engine.

This might be it.

His screams lift to the air when I pop open the trunk. "What the fuck are you doing? Where am I?"

"If you move, I'll kill you." I slip the sidearm out of my jacket to let him know that I'm not fucking around.

Watery blue eyes widen with fear as he lies in the trunk of his own car, and I hear a dull roar pounding in my ears. I raise the gun to his temple.

"Whoa, whoa, *whoa*! You can have my money." He grabs his wallet from his pocket and tosses it to me. It lands in a cloud of dust. "Just take it!"

Maybe I'll play with him before I eat him.

I grab the flimsy wallet from the ground and search through its contents. "Twenty bucks? That's all you got? Geez, a nurse's salary ain't much, is it?"

"I can get more! Please, don't hurt me!"

Don't hurt me. But the asshole didn't care about my brother, did he? He didn't give a flying *fuck* about him.

I grab the scruff of his neck and smash the heel of the gun over his face. His nose shatters and blood sprays all over his bright blue scrubs. A thrill shoots up my ribs as he clutches his face, moaning.

"Months ago you accepted a bribe from a man in the hospital. You were told to take a walk from the ICU. Don't fucking deny it!"

Terrified eyes glance at me. "I—I didn't."

I aim the gun at one of his knees and the cracking sound splits the sky, almost drowning out his agonized howl. Blood mushrooms around his knee and tears stream from his eyes.

"I bet that really fucking hurts, doesn't it?" Seized by a sudden burst of anger, I grab his blood-soaked knee and squeeze. He cries like a little bitch. "Answer me, you miserable prick!"

"Okay!" he screams, holding out his hand. "I did—some guy gave me money—"

My heart crashes against my ribs. "What the fuck did he look like?"

"I don't know! He had a suit—a black one. Thin face. Short black hair."

Jesus fucking Christ, this is useless. He could be describing John, for all I know, but the boss never does his own dirty work.

His voice raises an octave. "Look, I didn't know what was going to happen, okay? He told me to take a walk, so I did."

"Tell me how much they paid you for my brother's life."

He shakes his head, crying silently when he hears the rage trembling my voice. "I'm *sorry*."

"How much?"

The miserable bastard flinches at my yell. "F-five hundred."

My stomach sinks and I clench my eyes. Goddamn it. My chest tightens so that I can barely breathe. My brother's life was bought for five hundred dollars. They paid off witnesses and took care of the security cameras, but why would they leave this one breadcrumb for me to find? Sloppy. Not like John at all.

I can envision it. Several men in dark suits, silhouetted, quietly slipping into my brother's room. Grabbing the pillow behind his head and smothering his face. Mike wouldn't have been able to fight back in his condition. There's something about that—I want to throw up. A line of nausea creeps into my mouth as I imagine them digging it into his face. It would have been so simple. He was paralyzed.

"How does it feel to die for five hundred worthless dollars?"

"HELP!"

I cut off his screams with another crack. The bullet hits him square in the chest and his mouth bursts with blood. I fire again. Again. *Again.* So many fucking times. Until his body is riddled with holes and his blood pools in the trunk. I clean the gun with my shirt and then I toss it inside. Nathan's face is frozen in twisted agony, but my rage still burns. I slam the trunk lid down as the echoes of the gunshots fade in the distance.

I slam my fist into the car, warping the metal as my yells are swallowed by the mountain of crushed vehicles. I check my watch, my head pounding, and I grit my teeth.

Johnny's waiting for me at the MC.

Where I'm going to get engaged to some *bitch* I've never even met.

Great.

* * *

A sickening feeling possesses me like a slow-acting poison, unlike the fear settling in my guts. I stand in this dark room, waiting for Johnny to show up as François and Tommy eye me as though I'm a fucking liability.

I'm just waiting to die, aren't I?

This looks like just the place. Four walls. Suspiciously stained wooden floorboards. Two men eye-fucking me. We're way, way out in the boonies, in biker territory where no one will give a shit even if they hear my screams.

The door creaks, opening wide to admit a slim figure wearing a plain charcoal suit. It's Johnny, the boss of the family. Black waves of hair speckled with gray are rolled back to reveal a handsome face. Inwardly I recoil. He's the man who haunts my nightmares. I can't help but battle a burgeoning swell of rage and fear whenever I see him. The nausea goes straight to my gut.

Blood pounds in my head as I stare at him, conscious of the fact that if it weren't for him, Mike would still be alive.

He smooths his hands over his pinstripe suit, looking as immaculate as the devil as cold eyes scan my appearance. He glances at the men watching me.

"Leave us."

I dig my fingernails into my palms as François and Tommy push themselves off the wall and exit the room. The door shuts with a sort of hollow finality and we stare at each other for a moment. Iciness grips my stomach as Johnny strides forward, close enough to do anything he wants to me. His nostrils flare.

Is he sniffing me?

"You're drunk."

"Well, you didn't expect me to come here sober, did you?"

"Listen to me, you fucking moron. You're either going to jail, or you marry one of them. End of fucking story."

I might just rip my fist across Johnny's face. "I'm not going to marry some biker *cunt*. They put my brother in the hospital, or did you forget that?"

The boss bares his teeth. "I forget nothing. We were at war, Jack. Now we're not. It's that simple."

Piece of shit.

I want to scream at him that I know what he did. He's the most ruthless boss in history—he could have silenced my brother. They found cotton fibers in his nose and lungs. He suffocated to death, and I wasn't there. I wasn't there. The grief still tears at me like a hundred tiny knives cutting deep inside me.

It should have been me. I was the fuck-up.

The hatred boiling inside me must be plain on my face, because Johnny's eyes narrow dangerously.

"You have something you want to say to me?"

I would kill you if I had a shred of proof.

"Why the fuck don't you just kill me?" It bursts out of my mouth before I can take it back, the question finally ripped from my throat.

He clenches his fists. "What?"

"I know your style, Johnny. You don't give second chances. Why me? I'm Mike's worthless, ex-junkie brother. Why the fuck are you doing this for me?"

"You're my bargaining chip for this deal."

I let that sink in for a moment.

"Jesus."

Johnny approaches me, his face inches from mine. "I know you think I killed him. *I didn't.*"

I cross my arms, shaking my head as a painful grin stretches my face. "Sure."

I go flying as he shoves my chest. My back hits the wall and his fist slams into the space right beside my head.

"I had nothing to do with it!"

Earnest black eyes bore into mine. I study the creases in his face, feel his breath blowing hard over my face. I wish I could believe him.

"Fine."

"*Câlisse de tabarnak.*" He starts to turn away, then his snarling face screams at me again. "You're going to marry one of those girls, or you'll get your fucking death wish."

The sound of his screaming vibrates in my ears, almost painful. The airport heist fucked everything up. The CSIS went ape shit, even though the MC screwed us over and took the cash. Everyone needed alibis—everyone had one. Except for me. Anyway, nothing really mattered once Mike died. My brother was everything. Dead and gone. I couldn't deal with it. I expected Johnny to send someone to pop me, but he never did. I'm his only loose end. The only way to avoid jail is to marry the girl who's giving me an alibi. Spousal privilege. She can't testify against her husband.

Just kill me and get it over with.

It makes my stomach turn to think about marrying one of those fucking cunts. They beat my brother—hurt him so badly that he'd never walk again. They're accessories to his murder.

"Why the fuck are we making peace with these dogs?"

"I want my money," Johnny says baldly. "They're giving back most of the money from the heist, and I want things to calm down."

So that's it? They get to beat the shit out of Mike and everything is fucking hunky-dory?

"What about my brother?"

"They paid for hurting him. An eye for an eye."

They did. I saw the biker's body that Tommy tortured. It wasn't enough for me. Call me sick, but I wanted more.

"The new president knows we have the means to wipe them out, if we wanted. He wants peace, and frankly, so do I." Johnny runs a hand through his hair and steps away from me. "Let's go. I don't have all fucking day."

Die or marry some biker bitch. It's not really a choice, is it? If I go to jail, it won't be long before someone shanks me in prison. Johnny's willingness to do right by my brother would end the moment I posed a threat to him.

"This is fucking ridiculous."

Resigned, I follow Johnny outside the room back into the clubhouse, where a dozen or so bikers are waiting for us. The bloody struggle that started after we killed their president ended up with a more moderate, less reactionary leadership.

"They're just going to hand off one of their women to me?"

He gives me a look, warning me to silence. "They're desperate."

They must be to give one of their women to a guy who fucks around and gives no shits about it. The new president stands in the middle of the clubhouse, which looks significantly less shabby than the last time we came here. Gone are the stripper poles and the giant speakers blasting rock music. Thank fucking God. Behind their shoulders I see a row of women lined up like a cattle auction.

Sweet Jesus.

This is insane.

Johnny shakes the president's hand, who turns his oily gaze toward me.

The new president is a short, stout man with a russet-colored beard, which lightens in his heavy sideburns. His leather cut is cracked with age, but he wears it proudly. The look he gives me makes my teeth crack. The last thing I want is to marry one of these people. It's a fucking insult to my brother's memory. A *disgrace*.

It's temporary.

The president holds out his hand for me to shake, but I just can't stomach looking into that fucking asshole's eyes and taking his hand as though he's my equal. An image of Mike's lifeless body in the hospital bed flashes, and my face slowly burns. I feel like I can imagine it going black and curling backward, like that biker Tommy torched to avenge my brother.

That makes me smile.

I take his hand, and it's like a battle of who can crush the other guy first.

"These are the girls who are willing to provide an alibi for you."

Johnny crosses his arms. "If everyone keeps their mouth shut, we can put this behind us."

Cold rage brews in my chest as Johnny gives me a quelling look. *Put this behind us?* I look around for a friendly face, and see Sal, the underboss. He darkens as he meets my gaze and he very slightly shakes his head.

Don't do anything stupid.

Pissed, I turn back toward the women they have lined up for me. They stand close together, looking vaguely unhappy as they avoid my gaze.

Which one am I supposed to pick? The one who seems the happiest or the one I see myself fucking?

"So, what am I supposed to do once I pick one? Throw her over my shoulder and walk out?"

My humor echoes hollowly in the clubhouse and Johnny gives me a withering look before he turns his head.

"This is just a meeting," the president says, unsmiling.

Whatever.

My attention turns back to the row of women patiently waiting for me to make a decision. My eyes skip from pretty face to face, recognizing nothing but fear. I almost skip over the last one, too. Then my heart turns to stone. The long, highlighted blonde hair and deep-blue eyes strike me suddenly. That rosebud mouth was wrapped around my cock hours earlier. Holy shit, it's her. The girl I banged in the club. What was her name?

Beatrice.

Her eyes fasten on me and she does a double take, her sullen features gradually hardening into grim resoluteness.

So I already fucked the biker bitch.

Well, well, *well.*

This is interesting. Either she scoped me out or this is one hell of a coincidence. Considering the lack of surprise on her face, I'd guess it's the former.

Holy shit. Was does that mean?

Beatrice takes a small step back as I make a beeline toward her, ignoring the others. I stand a foot away from her, smelling the shampoo on her damp hair. Her pink lips, still flushed with the heat of the shower, look perfect. I want to wind my hand in her hair and crush those lips against mine. Without her makeup she looks even more vulnerable, though not as much as she did when she was naked under my hands.

Do not get hard right now.

Instead I just speak to her, almost trembling in anticipation. "I'd like a word with you in private."

She lifts her gaze, looking over my shoulder to the president as though for permission, which makes heat flare in my chest.

His gravelly voice cracks the silence. "Go, Beatrice. Take my office."

The girl who I fucked hours ago gives me a polite half-smile and walks toward a room across the hall. I open it for her and she walks inside, her limbs shaking. There's a small walnut desk and a couple chairs. She wraps her arms around herself as I shut the door and then the silence in the small room suffocates us.

I can't stop seeing her naked body. Mere hours ago she was completely and utterly mine. She clutches the edge of the desk, staring at me, and a sickening twist of self-disgust wrenches me. This girl represents everything I fucking hate, and I want to fuck her again.

"I didn't expect to see you again."

"It's *Jack,* right?"

She uses the French pronunciation for my name, the staccato sound clipping from her tongue. A deep, buried memory of my mother surfaces to my brain. She bends down from her chair, arms outstretched: *Jack, viens ici.*

She's gone, too.

"Yeah." My voice sounds unnecessarily loud in the small room. I approach her and she clings to that desk like it's life or death. I stop inches away from her. "What's the matter, sweetheart? You don't like being so close to me?"

Beatrice blinks her blonde lashes. "*No*," she says defensively. Then she looks up in horror. "I didn't mean that!"

Damn straight.

Fuck, she's hot. It's rare that a girl holds my interest like this, but I like the way she avoids my gaze and blushes prettily, just like a shy schoolgirl. I want to touch her, and I reach out to grab her shoulder, knowing she won't stop me. She trembles a little as I slide my hand to the base of her neck. I held her just like this when she sucked my cock. It tightens in my pants as her heady scent ensnares me like a strong shot of tequila.

"Why did you scope me out in that club? Don't deny it."

She glances at me. "They told me what they wanted me to do. I just wanted to see if I'd like you."

I guess that makes sense.

"From the way you were screaming, you seemed to like me a lot."

The ache pounds as a pink blush spreads over her cheeks.

"I made a mistake."

"You probably did." I rub her throat with my thumb. "Did you want to sample my cock again before sealing the deal?"

A shard of anger cuts at me as she meets my gaze.

"We can fuck in this room if you're still undecided—"

"Don't talk to me like that!"

I take a step back as she shoves my chest, looking furious. So the biker bitch has some personality after all. It's amusing to see the horror falling over her face, and I laugh at how frightened she looks.

My laughter dies and she stares at me with indignation.

"Why did you volunteer yourself for this?"

A defiant, hard look comes over her eyes. "None of your business."

"So much fucking attitude. You weren't like this at the club. You were *so eager* to be mine."

The little freckles on her nose burn, along with the rest of her face.

It's hell being so close to her. I grasp her neck lightly and feel her pulse jackhammering into my hand. She parts her lips and I can smell the mint on her breath. She even brushed her teeth to get the taste of my cock out of her mouth.

I can still taste her.

"Look, I made a mistake."

I don't give a fuck.

She makes a sudden movement with her hand. "I just wanted to make sure that you weren't a psycho. I didn't think it would go that far."

"Well, it did. I'm not crying over it."

My pulse races when I see how flustered she's getting. She seems tortured by that fact—and by my hands on her neck.

"Don't insult me by telling me you didn't like it."

"I did like it," she says, skin so bright that I can feel the heat. "That's not the point."

I lean over her so that she's pinned against me. Her panicked breaths blow on my lips and I dig my fingers into her hair. "I'm not crazy." A smile hitches up my face. "At least, not in the way you think I am. I'm not going to hurt you, but I'm sure as hell going to use you."

"What do you mean?"

"The MC wants to please me, so that'll be your job. *Pleasing me*."

"I—don't understand. This is about me giving you an alibi."

Hatred rushes into my throat. "This is about becoming my wife. Maintaining the alibi is just *one* of your duties."

"Maybe you should ask one of the others for this arrangement."

"I won't."

"Why?"

"Because I'm choosing you."

Her nostrils flare. "You didn't even *talk* to the others!"

"Do I look like I give a fuck about talking to some biker sluts?"

"They're not sluts—"

"I don't care. I hate them—I hate your whole fucking MC."

The injustice of it all boils up again, burning my throat. I fucking hate them—hate Johnny. The Devils MC got the drop on Mike and beat him. He was barely speaking and then someone finished him off. The MC wasn't involved. That nurse confirmed my suspicions.

"If you hate me then why go through with this?"

I feel the anger steaming off her skin. I lean in closer, even though she looks forbidding. Blood rushes to my head as I inhale the perfume of her skin, and I remember how it clung to me all the way home. Damn it, I'm getting hard just thinking about it. Fuck her. I tighten my fingers in her hair and crush my lips against hers, backing her against the desk. She opens her mouth in a gasp of surprise and I stick my tongue down the bitch's throat. She clings to my jacket but suddenly releases her hands as though she's been burned. I taste the mint in her mouth, but I want her to taste like me. I want to fucking defile this innocent biker girl.

You already did.

I pull back slightly. "I'll hate you, but I'll love fucking you."

Beatrice makes a face and steps away from me. Her chest burns a bright red and her hair is frayed. How far can I push her?

"Does the president know I've already tasted the goods?"

I practically hear the slap coming, and I deserve it, so I let her hand rip across my face. Damn, she's got an arm. She brings back her hand, and I'm distracted by how hot she looks when she's pissed off. Her hair whirls around her head as she comes in for another one, but I catch her skinny wrist in my hand and yank her forward. The gasp she makes when her body bumps into my chest goes straight to my dick. I remember her gasping just like that, with her arms like a vise around my neck, her tits in my face.

Fuck.

She flinches when my mouth hovers over her skin.

"I expect to see some of that fire in the bedroom."

"Go to hell!"

Then I let her go, laughing as she stumbles away from me to run back to her beloved clubhouse.

I am going to hell.

BEATRICE

What the hell is wrong with me?

I hit him. I *slapped* a made member of the Cravotta Crime Family—the family we're desperately trying to woo, the one that could literally crush this entire MC if they wanted.

Yeah, I just totally insulted one of their members.

My boots make a hollow sound as I pace in my bedroom, catching glimpses of my panicked expression in the dirty mirror hanging above my vanity.

I knew who he was when I found him at that club, but the moment he scooped me in his arms and demanded a kiss from me, he stopped being the mobster I was supposed to marry. He was just a hot guy at the club, and I wanted to feel his lips all over me. Those dark eyes. God, I wanted him the moment he made eye contact with me. His hands were all over me, so possessive and confident. There was whiskey on his tongue and I shivered at his unnaturally low, gritty voice. It was almost as if I could feel his words inside me.

I completely lost my fucking head the moment he told me to kiss him. Who does that? Who grabs a stranger's waist and demands that from them? He was irresistible. I just wanted to meet him before I agreed to sign away my life for a stranger.

In the coolness of my room, I wrap my arms around myself, trying not to imagine his hands stroking my body, his lips and tongue on my clit, his cock splitting me open and taking away what I saved for so long.

When they told me I might have to marry a made guy, I scouted him out. If I'm going to be married to some greaseball—probably for *years*—I should probably know what I'm getting myself into. Right?

I'm not the kind of girl who does one-night stands. Hell, I can count on my hand the number of times I've had sex. All my life I've been the good girl. Well, as close to good as I can get. Everything was for the MC. I waited and waited for Dad to find the right guy for me to marry. I waited for so long, and for what? So I could marry a man who hates me?

I'll hate you, but I'll love fucking you.

Unable to stand another second alone, I burst out of my room.

Someone has to know what I did—that I slapped the man and ruined the arrangement that was going to give us peace. Oh *fuck*. I am so goddamn stupid.

The door shuts, the sound echoing loudly. I step outside and walk down the hall, imagining eyes burning into the back of my head. Every creak I hear under my feet makes me cringe.

"Beatrice."

Shit.

Jett's voice rings out from a room that I almost walk past. It's not empty—filled with a couple of his men, who look at me with something more than cold disgust. Hope.

"Come inside, I want to talk to you."

The president's cutting gaze is like a javelin thrown to my stomach.

He wants to talk to me. Oh God.

Holding in my breath, I give him a nod and walk into his office, trying not to flinch when the door closes behind me. Jett surveys me over his desk.

"It looks like the Italian chose you."

The breath catches in my throat. "He—he did?"

"It hasn't been confirmed yet. Johnny says he wants to think it over for a while."

My fingernails bite into my palms as beads of sweat form on my skin. Jesus Christ, I can barely meet his gaze.

"This marriage is the best thing for the MC. I *hope* I don't have to explain to you how important it is that everyone keeps their end of the bargain. We can't afford another war with the Cravotta Family."

"So long as everyone shuts their mouths, we'll be fine," says Frank, who gives me a long, searching look.

"How long will I have to be with him?"

Pity wrinkles his eyes. "Until the investigation is over."

Well, fuck.

"If this marriage doesn't work out, don't bother coming back to the MC."

My heart thuds against my chest. "What?"

"I have no place for someone who supports a traitor—"

"I am *not* Maya!"

Three stunned faces turn toward me as my voice explodes in the middle of the room.

Oh my God. I just yelled at the president.

My face slowly burns, and I can just imagine the red creeping up my neck.

"You let her get together with the boss of the family, which started all this mess."

This again? How many times can I say that it wasn't my fault?

"Jett, you have to believe me. I wanted *nothing* to do with it—I am loyal to the MC—I've spent my whole life here." My eyes cloud over and burn. "*Please* don't send me away. Everyone I care about is here."

"Everyone? I've heard that you asked to visit Maya and her cock-sucking husband."

"She's my cousin! I just wanted—"

"No! You will not call her your cousin while you are under my roof. Good people died because your *cousin* wanted to fuck around with an Italian? That bitch is dead to me, and if you're not careful, you'll join her."

Tears slip down my cheeks, and I think again about how I utterly ruined my chances with Jack by slapping him. The president points at the door.

"Get the fuck out."

His voice rings in my ears as I practically run out of his office, a sob catching in my throat as I wipe my eyes. I walk into the main room in the clubhouse, which has a few people. Dad's not home, so I can't talk to him about this.

The wires hanging from the walls look like the entrails of an insect. The speakers were ripped out the moment Jett became president. The constant music was a distraction. He wanted an MC that was more focused. Business, not pleasure. The stripper poles and floorboards were next to go. He replaced them with dark, polished wood that show the scuffs of everyone's shoes.

I don't recognize this place anymore.

Everywhere I go, unfriendly eyes follow me. The heaviness from their glares presses down on my shoulders, and I think about my cousin, Maya. A flurry of complicated memories and emotions pass through my head: Maya combing my hair, her scissors trimming the length, mixing a batch of bleach for highlights. That awful smell always reminds me of her, and that time when she burnt my hair when she left the foil in for too long. We laughed about it, years later.

Now she's gone, and it's so lonely without her.

I miss her. I miss the sound of her voice and the fun we used to have. None of us are allowed to see her. She's a traitor—she fucked a man who was a barely tolerated enemy of the MC, the boss of the Cravotta Family. I heard through the grapevine that she had a baby boy. The seed of resentment that took root the moment she fled the MC grew into a bitter fruit. She left and I was stuck with the mess. I was dating Paul, and then he ditched me the moment the last president died. Everyone associated with Maya was shunned into nonexistence.

Fuck your dreams. Fuck what you want. Go see Jack now and beg for his forgiveness.

Or Jett just might have my throat cut.

* * *

I've never been outside by myself. Before yesterday I was completely naive to the world outside the MC. Just as fresh as a teenage kid, really.

I keep thinking that as I walk down the quiet suburban street, my footsteps sounding oddly loud as they echo down the strangely deserted sidewalk. I didn't expect to find him here, among a row of identical brownstones. St. Leonard is notorious for its Mafia ties, so I guess it's not that surprising. I just expected a little more glamor from a twenty-something party animal.

Whatever. Get in there and *grovel.*

Number 38.

I grab the metallic railing, which gives a rusty shriek as I climb the white steps to his apartment. For a moment my abdomen clenches and a vision of myself boarding a flight and flying far, far away grips me. My fist hammers the door.

The paralyzing seconds following my knock are the worst. Is he going to open the door and tell me to fuck off?

My insides feel like ice as I wait there as though held in suspension, but my thoughts keep racing. This is, bar none, the weirdest thing I've ever done. I'm here to beg a man who scares me and who I hardly know to marry me because I don't feel safe in my own home. A man who doesn't particularly make me feel safe.

I mean, Jesus.

Then a warped, dark shadow grows bigger in the glass, and the door creaks open to reveal a sliver of Jack. From what I can see of his face, he doesn't look happy.

"Hi." I don't know what else to say. He just stares at me, the one eye I can see blinking. "Jack, I—I wanted to apologize. Can I come in?"

In seconds the door opens and his hand shoots out, grabbing my wrist hard. He yanks me inside and slams the door shut, sending the bolts home. I'm crushed to his side as his hand gropes down my body, searching for weapons. His arm snakes around my neck, trapping me against his chest. Then he turns me around like I'm a doll and frisks me.

"Jesus!"

Finding nothing, he releases me roughly and steps back with a small smirk that makes my heart pound. "*Please.* Don't pretend that your heart isn't pounding because you're excited that I touched you."

He's a fucking ass, even though he's right. My heart is fit to burst, but that's more about being surprised than having his hands all over me. I clutch my chest and feel my skin jumping in my palm. I can't calm down, not with his heavy gaze all over me. A vivid memory of his hand squeezing my tits makes blood rush to my face. It's only been a day since we fucked, and the soreness between my legs suddenly pounds with warmth. Heat instantly rises to my cheeks and he smirks at me, dimples creasing into his face. He changed out of his suit into sweatpants, where I can just see the not so subtle bump between his legs, and a white tank top that shows off how cut he is.

"You came to this neighborhood alone?"

I nod, my eyes adjusting themselves to the darkness of his home. There are cardboard boxes everywhere, but the house looks lived in already—as if it belonged to his parents. Old picture frames hang on walls, photos of two boys—one significantly older than the other.

Jack follows my gaze and frowns, stepping in front of me as if to shield my view.

"Jack, I'm really sorry for—"

"Did you really come here to apologize?" He takes a giant step forward, jutting his hip into mine. Blood rushes to my head as his fingers sweep up my neck, and my back hits the door, temporarily knocking the air from my lungs.

"Or did you come here to have another round with this?"

He grabs himself, squeezing that mouthwatering bump.

My heart jumps in my chest when I notice the shape of him against his pants. My eyes linger there too long.

"See anything you like?"

I would like to slam my fist in your face.

"I didn't mean to hurt you."

A shadow crosses his eyes, turning his grin into a predatory smirk. "Yes, you did. It's okay. I like to think of it as foreplay."

It's hard to beg him when he acts like a complete jackass.

"I want this to work—I *need* this to work."

His eyes flash. "Why?"

For a moment I'm stunned by the intensity in his gaze. "I have my reasons."

"No," he says with so much force that I flinch. "That's not good enough."

What am I supposed to say? If I tell him the truth about the MC's threats, he won't give a shit.

"Maybe I want to get out of the MC. Maybe I want this."

"You want this?" he says with a bite of laughter. "You want to be my personal fuck-toy? Get down on your knees and suck my cock, then."

My face burns again. *I'm not going to get on my knees, asshole.*

"I've been wanting to leave for years."

Suddenly his demeanor changes tack with lightning speed from playful to terrifying. Harsh fingers dig in my hair and he suddenly yanks hard enough for tears to spring to my eyes.

"I call bullshit, sweetheart."

Jesus.

"I'm not lying!"

He grits his teeth. "Say that again, and I'll bend you over my knee."

"What the *hell* did I ever do to you?"

Then his breath hisses over my throat like the edge of a knife. "You're one of them."

The outrage from his voice makes me want to cringe. I've never felt like such a coward. He's an Italian, isn't he? A fucking *dago.* That's what they call them at the MC.

"I could say the same about *you.*"

"Except your MC ganged up on my brother and beat him until his legs stopped working."

A cold feeling spreads inside my chest like ice.

"He was your brother?" I can barely hear my own voice.

"Yeah."

I remember it now. My dad always tried to shelter me from what went on in the MC, but it was impossible after the mob crashed a truck into our gates with Julien's body strapped to the hood. It was retaliation for what the MC did to a man in the mob—I never knew his name.

"I'm sorry. Is he—?"

"He's dead," he says in a low voice, his energy dimmed.

I hate that I feel sorry for this bastard.

"What happened?"

Jack's fingers release my hair and he steps back, eyeing me curiously. "You have no fucking idea why they want you to do this for me, do you?"

Blood careens in my veins. "It's all about the alibi. You need one."

"They're doing it to placate me, sweetheart. Somebody killed my brother in a hospital. They want me to forget about it and move on." Then he runs his thumb over my lip. "So they sent a piece of ass to play with for a while."

A horrified gasp tightens my lungs and Jack gives me a sharp look. It pierces right through me. I don't know why the hell I'm so afraid, and then it hits me through a series of confusing images.

I was there.

I was visiting Bane in the hospital. There were lots of members in the ICU then. Through the window I saw three guys with leather cuts slip inside the room across from mine. Something about the way they acted made the hair rise on my neck. They were in and out. It couldn't have been more than five minutes. I assumed it was another member of the MC. Then later I heard screaming, "CODE BLUE!"

The man was dead. He was a wise guy. I didn't know what to think of it, but this must have been his brother.

They killed him. The MC I'm fighting to protect killed a man who couldn't even fight back. This is beyond the pale—unforgivable.

It's painful to meet Jack's gaze, but he doesn't seem to notice anything. His hands follow the slope of my shoulders and he plays with my spaghetti straps. He snaps them against my skin. Everything is confused—I'm numb with shock, but his hands won't let me forget my attraction to him, or my anger.

"I am *not* a piece of ass."

He makes an amused sound through his nose and then he pulls the straps down. A surge of rage suddenly hits my chest.

"You can't talk to me like that!"

"Oh yeah?"

His smirk incenses me.

"What're you going to do about it?"

Fucking smug asshole.

I'll show you what I'll do about it.

SLAP!

My hand rips across the side of his face and I feel the sting on my palm, breathing hard. His cheek flames red and then he turns back to me slowly.

Why the fuck— What the hell are you DOING?

Oh shit.

Then my breath catches in my throat as he digs his fingers in my hair, his mouth closing in. My body responds automatically to him, like a switch. Hot lips crash against mine and he sucks my lip in his mouth, giving me a hard nip with his teeth.

His other hand slides around my waist, pinning me to his rock-solid body. My heart flies in my chest like a bird. I can't help it. His tongue plays with me, and my hands slide up his chest, over the powerful, flat muscles. Then he breaks away from me, and I feel like I'm falling.

He loosens his hand from my hair and pushes it over my head so that I stumble down, catching his hips to break my fall. Then suddenly my mouth bumps against his thick cock and a tingle runs through my pussy.

"Be a good girl and suck my cock."

Heat flares in my chest as a dark chuckle shakes from Jack's mouth. He pulls down his sweats and his fully erect cock slides over my cheek. The hand at the back of my head pushes me so that I get a face full of dick. Fuck him, but it's hot.

I wrap my fingers around him and take him in my mouth as a small voice screams at me. This is fucked up. You shouldn't be letting him treat you like this.

He groans as he slides in my mouth. The pleasant taste of him fills my mouth as he grabs my hair and thrusts his hips.

"Swallow every drop of cum, and maybe you'll be lucky enough to become mine."

Asshole.

I shouldn't want to please this bastard, but then I take him in deep and he lets out a delicious moan that makes a pleasant wave run through my body. I grab his waist as he pumps into my mouth, making me gag as he buries himself. My tongue slides underneath him and swirls around his head. I love the feel of him inside me—the pulse of his heartbeat throbs in my mouth.

"Look at me," he says in a tight voice.

I look up into his red face, which trembles with urgency. I tighten my lips around him as my skin burns with need. He shudders and digs his fingers in my hair, exhaling a soft curse. I gag on his cock and pull him out, feeling how thick he is in my hands. My mouth swallows him again, and he bends his knees to fuck my mouth hard and fast.

"Take my fucking cum."

A thrill shoots up my chest as he buries himself deep enough to make me gag, holding himself there as he lets out a huge groan. My heart races as I realize what he's about to do—I've never done it before. His cock jumps and my mouth fills with warm, salty cum. I swallow it down quickly as he pulls back slightly and thrusts again, another load filling my mouth. It's fucking sloppy. How does he get me to do things I've never done with anyone else?

He slips from my mouth and my stomach tenses when he bends down and grabs my arms, pulling me upright. I wipe my lips as a smile twitches on his relaxed face. My arousal pounds though my body as he takes my hands and leads me to the couch. He sits down and yanks me, the same way he took me when I first met him. I tumble in his lap with a gasp and his laughter falls over my ears. Jesus, he's so warm. His head turns and his lips graze my forehead.

"I've had a lot of girls chase after my cock, but none of them were quite this determined."

What the hell am I doing?

"I've never done that with anyone."

"How did it feel?"

Another edge of anger digs into me like a knife. "Is this what you plan to do to me when we're married?"

"Yes. Over and over again."

At least he's honest.

"So this marriage is going to be fake?"

"Fake? You're putting on my ring. You'll be living in my house, sharing my bed."

The strangeness of it rings in my ears. Rough hands snake around my neck and jaw, forcing me to look into hungry eyes.

"So basically you want me to be a live-in whore."

His Adam's apple bobs up and down. "You'll be more than that."

It's clear from looking at his expression that "more" isn't that much. Great.

"I need to take you to Johnny. Give me a minute to get dressed."

Johnny?

"Now?"

"Yep," he says unhappily.

My insides do a backflip as I think about the ruthless mob boss. He's the same guy who killed and torched Julien, and left the burning corpse at our gate. My skin crawls when I remember seeing the blackened remains. It was retaliation, pure and simple, but it still made me sick to my stomach.

Johnny scares the shit out of me.

I stand up from the couch as I hear Jack retreat to his bedroom and strip from his clothes. The soft sound of them hitting the floor brings me a vivid image of his muscled body, covered in dark ink. I hang near the edge of his doorway and see a rich display of him tugging on a pair of black briefs over his amazing ass. Just the sight of his rippling arms and back makes my breath still.

Then his dark head turns around impassively, as if he senses my presence.

"I know I'm hot to look at and all, but it's a little weird if you're just standing there."

Damn him.

"We don't have to see Johnny. Just tell him I agreed to it."

Suspicion knits his eyebrows together as he walks to his closet and yanks out a fresh suit. He stares at me while shoving his legs through the slacks.

"We have to go see him."

I'm speechless as he finishes dressing, clearly oblivious to the fact that my limbs are shaking.

I follow him to the bathroom, where he's tucking in his shirt and running a comb haphazardly through his hair. His eyes find mine through the mirror.

"Please, Jack. I'm scared of him."

His expression doesn't change. "You should be. He's the devil."

* * *

The drive to *Le Zinc*, Johnny's notorious hangout, is torturous. Jack couldn't care less about me, so all I can do is clench my thighs and try to will myself to not be such a fucking coward.

Jack keeps shooting me glances filled with contempt.

"He's not going to touch you. If anything, he'll kill me. Stop being such a baby."

Small fucking comfort.

"Stop being such a jerk."

The car explodes with his laughter. It's so startling that I jump in my seat, and I look over incredulously to see him grinning from ear to ear.

"Bridget—"

"*Beatrice*!"

He smiles at me. "Beatrice, you're overreacting. He's not that bad."

I dig my nails into my knees. "You didn't get a charred corpse at the doorstep of your home. You didn't see it—"

His tone turns nasty. "Spare me, okay? I don't care about your beloved biker asshole. I don't want to hear about it!"

He's such a goddamn prick.

This is what my life is resigned to, I guess. Endless spats with a man who just wants to use me for my body. Seriously—he said it to my face.

I try to hold it together and then he stops his car a block from the restaurant. He turns off the engine and gets out of the car without a second glance, but I'm frozen in my seat. Sharp raps against the glass startle me and then he opens the door, a dark glare on his face.

"Let's go. I don't have time for this shit."

Calm the fuck down.

But I can't. The pressure between my eyes keeps building up. My life is a goddamn mess, and I've jumped into bed with a man who hates me. Who has a monster for a boss. My eyes burn and I keep them closed. My hands balls into fists. I dig my fucking nails into my skin.

I feel him reach across to unbuckle my safety belt.

"*Please*, Jack."

He relents, letting out a sigh. "Fearing men like John is pointless, sweetheart. If he wants you dead, you're dead. There's nothing you can do about it. *Nothing*."

His hand lifts to my face and gently wipes away my tears. It's the first time he's done anything remotely nice to me. Somehow that makes me well up.

"On my life, nothing will happen to you."

Like that means anything, coming from you.

I slide my hand into his and he helps me up, closing the car door behind me.

"It'll be fine."

Jack rubs my back briefly and then steps away, because his compassion has limits, I guess.

Le Zinc is a trendy place smack-dab in the hipster region of Montreal. Pristine white tablecloths cover every surface. Women in black cocktail dresses and pumps sit across from their dates in full view of the wide glass. Somewhere in that dark restaurant Johnny sits, surrounded by his entourage.

Jack grabs my upper arm, my skin tingling with electricity as he brings me close. It's as if he fears I'll turn tail and run. The hostess opens the door and nods at Jack, clearly recognizing him.

"*Bienvenue, Jack.*"

"*Bonsoir.* Same place?"

"*Oui. Après vous.*"

The hostess wears a floor-length glittering gown with thousands of black sequins. I'm horribly out of place in my knee-high boots and jeans.

His hand falls from my arm and I immediately miss it. Blood roars in my ears, the sound of the restaurant deafening. It's packed with people, which makes me feel a hell of a lot better.

Jack leads me away from the noise to a private room enclosed in glass. There he is, sitting at the far end of a long table with all of his captains. My heart squeezes with a sudden thrill when I see Maya, to his right. She cradles a baby in her arms. For a moment I stand there, watching the scene. Johnny's face cracks with a handsome, incredibly warm grin as the baby returns a heart-melting smile. He leans over and gives the baby a peck and then he grabs the back of Maya's neck and gives her a long, lingering kiss. She glows at him. God, they look happy. In love. It's way more than I hoped for.

"*Come on.*"

Jack's voice snaps me out of my trance and I follow him as he opens the door.

Oh fucking hell. I don't want to be here.

A dozen or so men look up from their meals and stare at me with bored expressions, except Johnny, who stands up from the table with a grin that reminds me of sharks.

"Johnny, sorry to disturb your supper."

He moves past me, leaving me at the far end of the table as he greets his boss with a kiss on both cheeks. Then he looks down the table at me and spreads his hands slightly.

Fine.

Stiffly I move down the table and Maya recognizes me, standing up with her baby.

"Beatrice!"

She ignores Johnny as she steps around him, her eyes already swimming with tears as she frees an arm to hug me. God, it's been so long since I've seen her.

"I've missed you." I wrap my arms around her and swallow the lump in my throat. "Sorry, I wasn't allowed to visit."

"I know," she says in a tight voice. Maya pulls away and the baby's fist wraps around my jacket, refusing to let go.

"This is Matteo."

Every thread of resentment I have toward Maya dissolves into air like lingering smoke as I look into his beaming face.

"Hi, Matteo!" I gently disengage his fist from my jacket, and he curls his fingers around my hand. "He's so sweet. Can I hold him?"

Maya nods, smiling widely, and then suddenly Johnny appears out of nowhere. Extreme distrust narrows his face and I back away from him, bumping into Jack's solid chest.

"Tommy, take my wife outside."

One of his captains, a lean, brutal-looking man, rises from his seat and nods.

"Sorry, ladies. We have business to discuss."

My heart falls as Maya gives me an apologetic smile. "We'll catch up later."

"Okay."

The joy from meeting my cousin's baby fizzles like a firework dud.

The mob boss gestures to his wife's vacant seat. "Sit."

Jack takes Tommy's place as the table resumes with conversation. He leans in over his boss's plate.

"She's agreed to go through with it."

Johnny nods as he picks up his fork and eats his plate of pasta, giving me a wary glance.

"I need you both to understand that the CSIS will suspect that this marriage is a sham."

"It *is* a sham."

"I know that, wiseass. They'll have people undercover, watching you. If there's even a shred of evidence, the whole fucking thing goes through. You will act like a couple. You will go on dates. We'll have a wedding with all your family, the whole shebang."

My fingers curl into the white tablecloth as a sullen look comes over Jack's face.

This was not what he expected.

"Not all the guests at the wedding will know."

"*Jesus*, John."

"What, you have a problem with this?"

"Yeah, I have a fucking problem. I didn't realize—"

Johnny's laughter cuts him off. "That what? You're going to be married to her for years. I hope you can learn to stand each other."

From the look on his face, not bloody likely.

He gives John a humorless smile. "Yeah. Fucking wonderful."

Years. We'll have to spend years pretending we're not miserable together. It almost makes me wish I had just taken a flight out of here.

"Jesus. It's not *that* bad."

"Really?" he snaps. "I'm marrying one of them."

His seething tone hits me square in the chest.

I don't want to marry you, either. Asshole.

"She won't be one of them once you're married. She'll be one of us."

Jack irons his face with his hands.

"It could be a lot worse. Suck it up and enjoy being out of jail."

I lean forward, choosing that moment to speak. "Will I get to visit my cousin?"

Johnny's smooth face turns toward me. "We'll see."

My chest deflates at the coolness in his voice. "When would we have the wedding?"

"As soon as possible. You need to get interviewed by the cops."

As soon as possible.

The clattering of knives and forks clashes in my ears, suddenly extremely loud. I stand up from the table without realizing it, blood roaring, the subtle thump of my heartbeat like ominous drums. Distantly I hear Johnny tell Jack that the wedding will take place a couple days from now. Jack shakes his hand and stands up again.

Jack slides an arm around my waist and leads me out of the room. We walk through the restaurant in a haze until finally we're outside and I breathe a gulp of fresh air.

I'll be married to the man I'm walking next to in a couple days. I want to feel better, but how can I when I'm with him?

We drive back to his place in complete silence. It's nearly 1:00 a.m. by the time we get back. My head reels from the meeting with Johnny. He parks his car in front of his brownstone and I follow him inside. My insides battle with my desire to get away from him and the fact that I really don't want to be alone right now.

I turn around as he locks the door, the sound sending a thrill through me. When he faces me, it's scary. He looks ready to kill, and he shrugs out of his jacket, hurling it to the floor. I'm afraid to touch him. To look at him.

"I'll see you when we get married." He lets me go with suspicion narrowing his eyes, and as soon as the door closes I feel it as though it happens inside me.

BEATRICE

My wedding day.

You know, the event some girls spend their whole lives imagining. The flowers. The dress. The cake.

All those details suddenly feel meaningless, like the vase of plastic flowers sitting on my vanity. What's the point of this charade? It's all *shit.*

"You can't do this."

I look up into the mirror, my eyes passing briefly over my joyless face to my right shoulder, where Dad sits beside me.

I never told him about Jett's threats, and I'm not sure that I should.

"It's done."

Anguish crumples my dad's face.

Please don't make this harder than it already is.

"We'll get you married to a nice man—a man in the MC."

A sigh blows out of my perfectly painted lips. "Daddy—"

"No! I won't see my only daughter handed off to some fucking *dago.*"

"He's not that bad," I lie.

"I want you to marry a man you're in love with, not to settle some score between the mob and the club."

I wanted that, too.

"I'm doing my part to help because I can't stand the thought of anyone else getting hurt."

I'm also trying to save my own ass.

Dad's face screws up in pain and he collapses in his hands, breaking with sobs.

Jesus.

Mary pauses in between doing my makeup as my father's crying echoes in the small room. I give her a sharp look and she puts the eyeliner down, retreating outside.

"Daddy, it'll be okay. Really, I'm fine with it."

My heart seizes when he grabs my arm, lifting his head. "It's not okay. I can't believe Jett asked you to do this before asking me."

"He's the president. He can do whatever he wants."

My dad gives me a long look before reaching into his back pocket and pulling out a lethal-looking switchblade. I recoil, but he takes my hands and presses the cool metal into my palm, closing my fingers around it.

"Daddy!"

"I want you to take this. I want you to promise me you'll use it if he hurts you."

Dad's red eyes bore holes into mine.

"He— I don't think he'll hurt me, Dad."

"The fact that you don't know for sure proves that you're in trouble."

My fingers close around the cold metal, my heart beating fast. Is he right?

"Promise me, Beatrice. I don't care what happens, I just want you to be safe."

My eyes slowly well up and Dad's face blurs in front of me, and then I wrap my arms around his neck. I'm scared, but I can't admit it. I'm not going to make Dad feel even worse about this.

"I'll send in your mother." He stands up, gently disengaging from my arms. "You look beautiful, Bea."

Mom doesn't even ask why I'm crying when she comes inside with the makeup artist. I look into the mirror, hating the sight of my swollen red eyes.

Fuck.

Finally the makeup is finished and I look like the most miserable bride ever. The guests, I keep reminding myself. They have no idea this is a sham.

A soft knock at the door twists my insides, and suddenly it opens to admit a man wearing a handsome tux. I stand up suddenly, knocking over a can of hairspray with my elbow. It clatters noisily on the wooden floor and Johnny smiles as it rolls up to his feet.

Fuck. What is he doing here?

"I'd like to have a word in private, if you don't mind."

Mom gives me an anxious look over Johnny's shoulder as she opens the door and disappears behind it, leaving me alone with him. Apprehension knots in my stomach as Johnny glances at the door as if to make sure it's shut, and then he gives me a warm smile that I distrust immediately.

"I—ah wanted to apologize for how I behaved at dinner the other night. My wife—your cousin—wasn't too happy with how I treated you. I'm sorry."

The knot in my stomach loosens slightly, but I don't stop white-knuckling the chair. I scan his smooth face. "It's okay."

Johnny smiles briefly before taking a chair beside the vanity and sitting down. He motions me to do the same. I sit down gingerly, my legs like springs. He takes the chair leisurely and places his hands on his knees, leaning in slightly.

"I also wanted to talk to you about your future husband."

God, that's what Jack is, isn't he?

"What about him?"

"I need this marriage to work. As long as both sides need each other, we'll have peace."

"Just as long as I stay with him."

Johnny doesn't miss the glumness in my voice. "I know he's a difficult guy—"

"You're wasting your time. I can't leave Jack any more than he can leave me. The MC cut me off."

He bows his head, hiding his surprise. "I'm sorry to hear that."

No, you're not.

"If everything goes well, maybe you can visit Maya on a regular basis."

"The Maya I knew never needed permission to hang out with her family."

He clasps his hands together as a smirk widens his face. "That was before she got married to me."

Screw you.

"Stop acting like I'm the bad guy. Our families were at war, and I don't trust you yet. I can't have you around my son."

I bristle instantly. "I would never do anything to hurt a child!"

"It's nothing personal."

Like hell it is!

"You have no idea what it's like to be a parent."

I want to break something. "Why the hell are you here?"

"To give you an incentive, hon. Help me calm Jack down, and I promise you time with my wife and our son."

My heart crashes against my ribs. I miss her— God, she's the only friend I have now. "What do you mean, 'Calm him down?'"

"Jack's been going through some rough times after the death of his brother."

Blood rushes to my head at the mention of him. The men wearing leather cuts. One of them looked both ways down the hall before entering the room, which was dark. The nurse's screams still echo in my ears.

Jesus fucking Christ.

"I'm hoping that having a wife will take the edge off some of his behavior."

"He—he really wants to find out who did it."

"Yeah, I'm looking into it."

Johnny's voice blackens and a pain hits me square in the chest. If they knew what I knew, there would be no mercy. From both sides. I swallow hard and force myself to look at John.

"Anyway, just get close to him. Calm him the fuck down. I'm not expecting a miracle, but I'd really appreciate it."

I give him a stiff nod. "I'll try."

I doubt I'll be able to make a dent in his behavior.

Smiling, Johnny stands up just as the wedding march begins, and my stomach takes a sickening turn. My throat thickens and I brace myself on the vanity, breathing in deep, shuddering breaths.

"Oh shit. It's starting." His grin falters as he watches my face. "All right, I'll get out of here. Congratulations," he adds quickly.

"Thanks," I say as he disappears behind the door.

I stand up, shaking as I hold the bouquet. Jesus. Why did I agree to do this? And why the fuck did we have to have such a big wedding?

I enter the room where all my bridesmaids are waiting for me. Maya, my maid of honor, squeezes my hand right before she leaves. Then the doors open and my dad appears at my elbow and I'm half hoping that Jack fled, but he's right there. He's wearing a gorgeous tux with a bright-yellow handkerchief in his pocket, just like the flowers I'm holding.

Don't faint.

Everyone stares as I make my way down the aisle, and I wish that I could vanish on the spot. What a fucking nightmare. It's all constructed—the flowers, the priest, even the groom standing at the altar, looking like he'd rather be anywhere but here. Dad gives me away and Maya takes my bouquet, and then there's nothing between Jack and I. His face looks drawn in and pale, as if he spent last night drinking. Can't say I blame him.

I barely listen to the priest, only remembering when I'm supposed to nod and mutter meaningless phrases. Jack says something about "pledging my eternal love," which we both know is bullshit. He slides a ring on my hand and then his clean-shaven face comes within centimeters of mine. The moment I feel his breath on my lips I lean forward, irresistibly drawn to the taste of him. Shocks of pleasure zap down my spine as he kisses me. The crowd screams with delight. Before I can really savor it he breaks away, blanched. We walk down the aisle, hand in hand.

Holy fuck, we're married.

The chaos follows us all the way to the street, but the whole thing is so dispassionate. Every movement is calculated. Jack opens the door to a Mercedes and I climb into the backseat, picking up my dress. He turns and waves to the others, and his smile disappears the moment he joins me. My ears still roar with everyone's cheers. They echo inside me hollowly.

Jack looks ill at ease. I think about Johnny's plea and I look at my surly, discontent husband. I'll have a better chance taming a lion than him.

We sit in silence for a few minutes.

"I need a drink."

He almost gives me a smile. Then he digs the champagne from the ice bucket in the backseat. The cork pops loudly and he shakily pours two flutes of bubbly, golden liquid, handing one to me.

"Congratulations, I guess."

I guess.

We clink glasses in what must be one of the most depressing

cheers ever and then we drink. Jack inhales his glass. My nerves refuse to flatten, even as Jack pours a second drink for me and I gulp that down, too. I hold mine out for another, but he shakes his head.

"There's nothing more tacky than a drunk bride."

"So you can get drunk but I can't?"

He grins as he downs another glass. "I can hold my liquor."

'Cause you're a drunk.

"It's the only way I'm going to get through tonight."

"And what about me?" I begin in a heated voice. "How am I going to get through it?"

Jack sets his drink down and slides over the seat so that his thigh presses against mine. I feel the shock of his touch like an electric jolt. His mouth breathes over my ear. "You'll get through it and make me look good, or you'll be punished when we get home."

I look at the ring glittering on my finger. It's beautiful, but everything feels so wrong. Every dream I had about my life is destroyed, and I did it to myself.

"Jack, I need to know that everything will be all right. *Please.* I can't do this unless—"

"—Everything will be all right," he says, deadpan. "Do you feel better now?"

No.

"You should. This is the best thing that could happen to someone like *you.*"

"What the hell does that mean?"

"You're out of the MC."

"Assuming we don't get divorced or this alliance blows up in our faces."

"Yeah. In that case, you'd be fucked."

Hating him, I slide down the seat to get away from his touch. How can Johnny expect me to have any sort of influence on this man? He doesn't fucking care about me. At all. I might as well be a piece of furniture in his house.

I can't stand him, and he hates me. What a promising start to our marriage.

The car stops and I take his hand as he helps me up, a fake, beaming smile on his face.

Fuck you.

The reception hall is just a giant, windowless room. I'm grateful that we have a sweetheart table to ourselves so that we can hate each other privately, but it's still awful.

I sit down next to him. He's the picture of what the perfect husband should look like. His brown hair is rolled back into gentle waves, exposing his face. He's rough and angular, but he has a heart-stopping smile that makes butterflies flutter in my stomach. There might've been joy in those brown eyes once, but it's long gone by now. He's a beautiful, bitter shell. In pain. He grabs his glass of wine and drinks and drinks, surrounded by people he despises. The guilt surfaces again, and this time it's worse because we're married.

I know who killed his brother.

He smiles when everyone clinks their forks to their glasses and then he turns to take my face in his hands. Gentle lips touch mine and a fiery jolt hits my core. It would steal my breath away if I didn't know that it was pissing him off. We break away and sit back in our seats.

"Look at that fucking jerk." He points to Johnny, who gives him a wide grin as he joins in with the heckling.

"You have to stop talking like that! He's the boss."

Jack looks like he wants to say something, but he holds back, tipping a larger gulp of wine down his throat. Then he grabs me again to kiss me, and they shut up.

It's a fucking nightmare of an evening.

I smile until my teeth hurt, picking up my dress to dance with Jack on the floor. He looks completely checked out. The alcohol makes him fluid, but I'm still a nervous wreck. When we return to our seats, the clinking and hooting starts again and I'm about three seconds away from losing it. My face stretches and I'm trying to smile. *Smile*, damn it.

A heavy arm suddenly lies on my shoulders, and Jack grasps my hand under the table, giving me a squeeze.

"Just think of it as a party."

"This is worse than I imagined."

Jack gives me a grim sort of smile, which grates when the clinking starts again.

"That's fucking it!" he roars.

He stands up, looking like he's out for blood.

"Get up."

"Where are we going?"

I stand up with him and he grabs me hand, and I'm surprised at how purposely he strides forward, given how fucked up he must be. We walk right past all the clinking glasses and silverware, and right out of the reception hall.

Jack cranes his neck, looking down the halls for an escape. "Here."

"We can't just leave."

"It's my wedding. I can do whatever the fuck I want."

He tugs me along and I follow him, my heels noisy on the marble floor.

"In here."

He pulls me through a set of double doors, leading us straight into the busy kitchen. Cooks wheel their heads around to see the bride and groom standing in the middle of the stainless steel room.

"What the hell are we doing here?"

"Finding somewhere quiet…and private."

I don't trust the wicked grin that flashes on his face as he reaches in a tall jar and grabs a long wooden spoon.

The head chef approaches Jack, who takes a few hundred-dollar bills and slips them quietly in his hand. "If anyone disturbs us, I'll shove a gravy boat up your ass."

Then he opens a door to the pantry and tugs me inside, closing the door in the chef's bewildered face.

"What the fuck are we doing here?"

Jack taps his side with the wooden spoon, which I eye warily. "You ask too many questions."

He's in a weird mood. I back up, passing rows of dried pasta and cans of vegetables until my back hits the wall.

"Give me your body, sweetheart. I'm going to take you right now."

He closes the space between us, and my heart jumps into overdrive as he slides his arm around the back of my neck and draws me into his body. I lift my head up, unable to resist the authority ringing from his voice—the cologne he wears, so male and aquatic, rolls over me like the alcohol we drank. Then I kiss him, sealing my lips against his. He reaches behind me, undoing the laced-up back as his tongue slides inside my mouth. His fingers burn my skin when the back peels away.

"Fuck. Look at you."

But I'm looking at him, and my mouth waters at the raised bump in his slacks. I reach for it, my palm flattening against his rock-hard cock as he pulls my dress down. It slides over my breasts, which he gives a quick kiss, then down my stomach and to the lacey panties I bought. His fingers scratch me slightly as he drags over my bony hips, and then I gasp as I feel the warmth of his tongue briefly on my pussy.

I'm completely naked.

He straightens as I bend down, stepping out of my wedding dress and carefully folding it on cans of soup.

"You're really going to fuck me in a pantry?"

His slightly damp hand grabs the back of my neck as lust invigorates his movements. "I'll fuck you wherever and whenever I want."

My muscles twitch as I feel the wooden, flat surface of the spoon gently tap my ass.

Why am I letting him do this to me in a pantry in the middle of a kitchen, of all places?

I can't answer that. All I've been thinking about these past few days is being filled by him, the very breath knocked out of my lungs with his powerful thrusts, and how damn good it felt.

I touch his chest and undo some of his buttons, but he makes a tutting sound and pulls my hands away.

Roughness grates Jack's voice. "You're going to get on your knees and you're going to suck my dick."

The wooden spoon taps my shoulder, and I feel a sudden urge to seize it from him and whack him over the head with it.

"Either you do as I say, or we go back out there. Let's face it, you're going to have a better time sucking me off than attending your own wedding."

True.

Somehow this dirty shit really *does* get me excited, or maybe it's the fact that the last time I had sex was a couple days ago and it's all I can fucking think about.

A smirk tightens his face as I slowly drop to my knees.

"That's a good girl."

It's condescending as fuck, but some sick part of me likes the amusement in his voice.

The belt unloops from his slacks and it slides in his hands. He lets it fall to the floor with a loud jingle and then slides down his pants, rolling his dark briefs over his thick cock.

"Did you miss it?"

He grasps the back of my neck, and my lips bump against the pearly sheen over his head. Damn it, it turns me on to see how hard he is.

"Did you spend the last two days touching yourself, wishing you had something bigger to fill your tight cunt?"

His husky voice strikes me right to my core, and then his fingers tighten in my hair, demanding a response.

I raise my head and meet his gaze, wrapping my hand around him. "Yes, I did."

Then he takes the wooden spoon, stroking a line from my ass, up my back and neck. The coarse wood presses against my cheek. I follow its pressure, turning my head against his shaft. Then my lips open and he slides in with a small groan. His cock buries deep in my throat, his blood pulsing hard through the vein throbbing on his shaft. It turns me on to feel him getting into it. My heart pounds against my chest as he starts thrusting.

"I love your mouth when it's stuffed with my cock. You have no idea how hot you look right now."

He pulses in my mouth and then suddenly I feel a sharp sting on my ass. Jack grins at me, the wooden spoon tight in his fist.

Did he fucking spank me with that thing?

The round shape of the spoon burns on my skin.

I fist his cock and slide him out of my mouth. "What the hell are you doing?"

"I told you to suck my cock."

He reaches down and grabs himself, aiming between my lips and groaning loudly when I take him in again. He doesn't miss a beat and rams himself hard enough to make me gag.

He fucks my mouth, occasionally ripping that wooden spoon across my ass. It burns like a son of a bitch, but I'm thrilled. He just can't help himself.

I swirl my tongue underneath his shaft, spreading my mouth wide as he pulses inside me. I grab his muscular thighs and slide my hands up, grabbing his firm ass. I know it's fucking insane that I'm giving my husband a blowjob in this pantry, but holy shit, it's so hot. I can forget that we're here when he moans loud enough for the cooks outside to hear us. I can even forget that I can't stand him.

Suddenly he pulls my head away from his body and he slides out of my mouth. His face twists as if in agony and then he pulls me upright. His arm wraps around my tits as his cock slides between my legs. My legs tighten around him, my back against his body as his breath billows over my neck.

"Show me how much you want it. Show me how much of a cock-hungry slut you are."

Holy fuck.

My clit is on fire as he gently thrusts and I watch his cock slide in and out between my thighs, slick with my juice. My head wrenches to the side and his hot lips crash against mine. I just want to turn around and slam him against the wall. I'm so worked up, and he keeps groping my tits and squeezing my nipples. Somehow his roughness on that sensitive area feels so fucking good, and I buck against his cock.

My pussy rides against his shaft as I bend over and grind on him. He gives a groan that vibrates through my body, striking my core.

"That's it."

He places a hand on top of mine, which grabs his head, and presses down so that he rubs harder on my clit. A moan shakes from my chest and he plants a wet kiss on my neck.

"That's it baby, moan for me. Tell me how badly you want it."

I arch my back against his, clenching over and over again. Holy fuck, I just want to nudge his cock up a little and feel his head pierce me like it did the first time.

"Please, Jack!"

His teeth bite down on my neck as he does a brutal thrust against my clit. "Your cunt needs a bit of stretching before I fill you up again."

His fingers slip down, curving around my mound before he pierces through. My body gives a violent twitch as he enters me, stroking his fingers against my raw clit. My muscles clench around him as every sensitive part of me feels like it's on fire. He moves his fingers to each side, stretching me out.

"Jack, I want you inside me. I need you right now!"

He lets out something that's halfway between a hiss and a groan. Another finger slides in, and I bite my lip against the pressure. He slips away and I hear a plastic, tearing sound. Then I see him rolling a condom over his cock.

"Shit."

Then he pushes me forward so that my arms grab the shelves, knocking over cans. My heart gallops ahead as he adjusts his cock and his fingers slip out of my pussy. There's a slight pressure and then our sighs mingle in the air. It feels fucking huge, just like last time. Breath squeezes out of my lungs as he anchors himself. It's still a foreign thing—feeling a man inside me. But his hands squeeze my hips as he digs himself a little deeper and he rubs against my clit, sending electrical shocks up my spine.

He's incredibly warm, and I miss his hardness as he pulls back before rutting me deep. Again and again. Hard enough to knock things off the shelves. He fucks me so hard, I forget myself. I don't even remember my own name. Oh God. It's just the most incredible thing. He's incredible.

He makes sounds I've never heard from a man. Deep, rasping groans. He pinches the flesh on my ass and smacks me hard and then he reaches around me, grabbing my tits to hoist me upright, still buried.

Wordless, he slips out of me and turns my shoulders around. Then he hoists me in his arms and shoves my back against the wall. I throw my arms around him and wrap my legs around his waist. I get to see his face as his cock slides in. His hair sticks to his neck and his teeth are clenched together. He explodes with moans, gasping hard as he rams me against the wall, and I don't think I've ever seen anything so beautiful. I kiss him and he bites my bottom lip. Pressure builds inside my pussy, the thick shaft rubbing against me like the friction needed to start a fire. I'm close to it—I feel it. I dig my nails in the back of his neck and gasp when our lips break away. Then he shakes with a huge yell and thrusts so hard I can feel every inch of him, all the contours. Jack's arms shake as energy pools from his limbs, and he pulses, breathing hard. Then my own explosion rocks me, and I find his lips again. I want to taste him. He swirls in my mouth as we both lower to the floor, exhausted.

We stay intertwined for a while. It feels sweet, like my first time with him. Jack nuzzles my neck and blows gusts of air. The glow radiates through my skin, and I just want to sit in his arms for a while.

The happy moment bursts the moment the door shakes with a loud series of bangs.

Jack raises his head and roars, "Fuck off!"

A voice dripping with acid filters through the door. "It's Johnny. Get the fuck back to the hall, *now*."

Oh my fucking God.

"Fun's over," I say in a low voice as his footsteps disappear.

"Yeah."

The chill from Jack's voice freezes over the temporary warmth between us. I watch him retreat back into his shell. His eyes close like shutters on windows and he disengages his arms from me, as though in pain. It twists inside me like a tiny dagger in my heart. God, how long will I have to do this?

Jack picks himself off the ground, already turning away from me as though I don't matter. It takes at least fifteen minutes to put the dress back on and then we rejoin the hall.

Another excruciating hour later and hundreds of guests demanding a dance, a kiss, a whatever, we're allowed to tear ourselves from the reception. Then it takes another hour to thank everyone for coming, and then finally we're allowed to leave.

I look up at those white steps to his apartment. My home.

"I guess I live here now."

"I guess."

Neither of us sounds very excited at that prospect.

He opens the door for me and I hobble up the steps with his help. Once we're inside, Jack slams the door and locks it.

"There's a spare bedroom down the hall to your left."

He vanishes from my side like a ghost. An hour later I have the dress and makeup off, and I lie down in this strange bed. I'm too wired to sleep, and part of me feels a tiny prick of pain at being so carelessly tossed aside.

It's the loneliest night of my life.

JACK

I wake up in a state of agitation. The sheets cling to my skin, drenched with sweat. Heart-pounding dread. The cold, clammy feeling follows me as I rip off the sheets and stand from the bed. I run fingers through my damp hair. What's missing?

I tear through drawer after drawer, throwing their contents on the floor. My feet slip on pairs of boxers. What am I looking for? I don't know. The irrevocable sense of loss yawns inside me. It has to be here somewhere.

It's oddly bright. Everything has a blue sort of haze. I stride into the kitchen, feeling a swell of disappointment as I open cabinet doors. The fridge holds nothing of interest, and I slam it shut.

Blood careens through my veins. I dive to the couch and fling the cushions aside. I don't know how to explain it. Something's gone. Something dear to me.

"Where are you?"

My fingers tear through the fabric, and my throat starts to close.

"Where the fuck are you?"

I straighten, my limbs shaking as I look around the deserted apartment. The chill moves up my chest, seeping inside, moving its icy tendrils around my heart. I can't find him. I can't—

I'm in a parking lot. Dark shadows shift in front of me, their forms obliterated by the bright white behind them. Then an arm suddenly slides across my neck and chokes off my air. I tug at his arm, but I'm so goddamn weak. Then the shadowy form in front of me steps forward, and I recognize John's face as blackness creeps around the edge of my vision.

"Too close, Jack."

The cold voice settles in my chest like ice. My fingernails drag in his tough skin as a smile lifts the corner of John's mouth. The man's arm crushes my windpipe and I fall down, my lungs burning. My face kisses the concrete and then suddenly air returns to my lungs.

What the fuck?

I pull back and feel wetness on my lips. A woman's mouth. I'm lying on soft sheets, and there's a naked blonde underneath me. Beatrice searches me with her deep-blue eyes and runs her fingers though my hair. I sink down and kiss the dusting of freckles right under her eye. My cock twitches when she wraps her arms around me, and I nuzzle her neck, feeling her stomach jump as I kiss her.

"Jack."

Something pierces through my back. I feel the sharp edges digging through my muscles and tearing sinew as I collapse over her body. Her arm strains, and the object rips out of my back. The fucking pain. That innocent smile plays on her lips as I roll off her. She straddles my hips and lifts the blade dripping with blood in her hands. Still wearing the same smile, she plunges down—

My eyes snap open to a blank ceiling, and a surge of energy hits me square in the chest. I gasp out loud, heart still galloping ahead. I sit bolt upright as the sheets stick to my skin.

What the *fuck* was that?

I wipe the sweat from my brow as my body radiates with lingering phantom pain. The sheets whip around my legs as I tear them off and stand upright, walking through the door of my bedroom—Mike's old room—and into the kitchen. The bottle of scotch in the kitchen cabinet burns in my head. My mouth waters. I want it so fucking badly that I can feel the richness rolling on my tongue. My legs move of their own accord. I see myself opening the cabinet door, grabbing the bottle, and slamming a glass on the table. It's then that I notice the wedding band.

Jesus Christ. I totally forgot.

I'm married to a biker bitch.

I forget the bottle of scotch and stride to the guest bedroom. My hand grasps the door handle and I turn—fuck, it's locked. A crazed, leaping feeling makes me hammer the door. She could be doing anything in there. Then I crash my shoulder against the door and splinters of wood fly everywhere. The dream fills my head with venom. I don't trust the bitch—I'm going to put her in her fucking place.

The door swings wide open and I see Beatrice backed up against the headboard, her hair mussed around her head and her blue eyes wide.

I approach the bed, watching how the t-shirt she's wearing rides up her thighs. A sliver of pink panties through her locked legs makes my cock twitch.

"Rule number fucking one. No locked doors while you're in this house."

She clutches her chest. I can see her heart fluttering the white t-shirt she's wearing and the soft outline of her tits, her nipples gently peaking the fabric. Then I remember the promise I made to use her body as long as she was mine as blood pounds in my head.

"*You could have knocked.*"

"I don't trust you, sweetheart."

The mattress squeaks as I sit down beside her. There's really nothing stopping me from ripping that t-shirt from her body. It's one of mine. I realize that with a sudden, hot thrill that leads straight to my cock.

"What exactly do you think I'm going to do to you?"

"Stab me in my sleep with the switchblade you stuck in your wedding dress?"

She drains of color and her mouth hangs open, apparently struck dumb. "M-my dad gave it to me. I would've never—"

"Go ahead and try it. I'd enjoy tying up your arms to my bedpost and leaving you there until I've had my fill of pussy."

"Jack, I would never do anything—"

"Second. If you fuck me over, I'll fuck you. Then I'll throw you out like a used condom."

She flinches at the heat in my voice, her skin the color of a pale rose. "Okay."

"Third rule. Don't touch my shit. If I catch you nosing through my belongings, I spank your bare ass until it glows bright red. Understand?"

I love how she sits up straight backed and nods at me like a good little girl. I cup her face with one hand, and she lets out a sigh.

"Good wives obey their husbands," I say, fighting to keep the laughter out of my voice. "I need obedience from you."

Her eyes flash and her voice carries a hint of defiance. "I thought you didn't want a wife."

I rake my fingers up her neck and fist her hair, yanking so that her neck arches over my wrist. Fuck, it's hot. I can see her hard nipples poking the white t-shirt. She lets out a painful hiss.

"Ow!"

"If you're going to give me a smart mouth, I'll put you in your place. I have no problem doing this in public."

She flushes violently. "No, please don't!"

I want to laugh at how terrified she looks. Damn, maybe this won't be too bad. I palm her stomach, slipping my hand under her t-shirt. She lets out a breath. My hand sweeps up her abdomen until I grab ahold of one of her nice tits, squeezing her nipple with my thumb and forefinger. A moan shakes from her throat that sends blood rushing to my cock.

I bend my lips to her ear, loving how she shivers when she hears my voice. "Next rule. No panties in the house. Take them off now."

Beatrice turns her head, her mouth parted. She wants me to kiss her. I want to. I want to bite her fucking lip, especially when she looks at me with that leaden expression.

"Don't make me repeat myself."

Without a second's hesitation she hooks her fingers under her panties and slides them down her ass. She rolls them from her hips and I see the sheen of juice over her pussy. The panties scrape against her long legs until finally they pool around her feet. I lift them up and ball her panties in my hand, throwing them across the room.

Beatrice clings to the bars on the headboard, knees firmly held together as her fingers curl around the metal. The shadow of her tits moves behind the shirt, sending another jolt to my cock. I grab her waist and slip my hands underneath her shirt, lifting it over those beautiful, perky tits. She tilts back her head as I pull it over her. Then her silky hair falls over her shoulders like beaten gold. Beatrice looks as fragile as the night I met her.

I take her by the throat and set her down on the bed, her hair spilling around her like a halo. My cock strains against my pants, throbbing so hard that I grind my teeth together to ignore it. She sucks in her lip and bites it. Fucking hot.

Slowly I tug down my briefs, releasing my length from the tight fabric. I grab the base of my cock and pump it a few times. Pre-cum dribbles out of the tip to slide down. She watches me with unmistakable greed.

"You just love taking orders, don't you?"

She's like a red traffic light, burning on cue. My thumb strokes her neck and she opens her mouth, apparently speechless.

"You don't care about what I love."

She turns her head to the side and pretends as though her cunt isn't dripping and her heart isn't racing from being so close to me. I take her legs and force them apart, revealing her glistening pussy.

"You're right. I don't."

I've never felt her bare pussy on my cock, and I decide that I want to make her suffer for talking back. So I slide between her legs and touch the tip of my head against her wet cunt. I grunt as I feel the warmth sliding around my head, suppressing the urge to dive in and surround my cock with tight pussy. She lifts her head and shudders with a small moan. Then I slide my cock up, massaging her swollen nub. I grab her thighs and slowly inch my way between her legs. My fingers glide up and make an arc inside her. She makes a high sound that turns me on—it's like a stroke to my dick.

"I'm not going to allow you to come anymore. Not without my permission. That's the last rule."

She arches her back, her muscles clenching hard around my fingers as I slide them out. I grab myself and move between her lips, stroking that sensitive clit as gently as possible.

"But I can't control it!"

"You will, or you'll be punished."

Her thighs tremble as I insert two fingers back into her warmth as I tease her with my cock. With my other hand I stroke myself. I fist my cock, feeding the pressure building behind my balls. Her breaths become labored, hitching into a high groan. She bucks against my hand and I feel like I'm going a little crazy, too. Her wetness is all over me and all I'd have to do is move my cock a few centimeters down.

"Can I come?"

"*No.*"

I fight a smile as her face twists with agony and bury my three fingers deep in her cunt, rubbing her nub hard. All I have to do is watch her tits spilling over her chest and that beautiful pussy open for me, just waiting for a nice, thick cock. Flaming heat licks my balls, my hand making friction with my dick. The ache intensifies with every desperate look thrown my way. When her soft moans hit my ears, a surge of energy runs down my length. My hand moves up and down my throbbing cock, faster and faster. Then my balls tighten and move up, the pressure finally releasing like the blast of a gun. Thick ropes of cum shoot out, draping over her tits. I pump furiously as ecstasy washes over me, still fucking her with my other hand. More jets of cum fly out, sticking to her pearly-white skin. Good fucking God, it's incredibly hot. I keep fisting my cock until every drop of lands on her.

She turns toward me, flushed, waiting for my approval. A sick part of me loves how easily she submits to me. She was probably born and bred for this. I can only imagine the bullshit they must have taught her at the MC—obey your father and stay pure. Girls with pure vaginas go to heaven. I wonder how much pussy I sent to hell with my dick.

"You can come now."

My cock is still hard, so I aim my head right behind her swollen pussy and I shove through, pinching her clit. Beatrice cries out and comes hard on my dick. I grab the back of her head and claim her sweet mouth. She kisses me back, pausing to moan in my mouth. I ride the wave of both our orgasms until my eyes feel heavy.

She sprawls out underneath me as redness pricks across her skin. I take the balled-up t-shirt and wipe the cum from her body and then I move to get up from the bed, but she tugs at my arm. The haunted look from her pure blue eyes stops me. Her fingers are surprisingly strong around my arm. She wants me to stay—to fucking *cuddle*.

For a moment I consider shutting her ass down, but her eyes tug at me. I roll back into bed with a sigh and I wrap an arm around her shoulders, curling her body into my chest. It feels good to have her weight against me, so much that I close my eyes and feel myself drifting off.

"Jack?"

"Hm?"

"What do I get out of this?"

I open my eyes, smiling as I catch her gaze. "You get me."

A shadow falls over her eyes and I feel a small knife in my chest.

"But it doesn't mean anything."

"Do you think Johnny would insist on a traditional wedding if it didn't mean something? You're wearing my ring. You're living in my house."

"Only until this investigation is over."

"Which will take years."

It's like a hammer dropping on an anvil, loud and harsh. I try thinking of years of this: bitter resentment, fights, and frequent, hot sex.

Her body moves in my arms and suddenly I'm face-to-face with her. Her eyes are so blue.

"What am I, Jack? Am I some girl you get to fuck whenever you want? Am I a biker bitch?"

You're my wife, I think automatically, but the words fail to sink in. She's still one of them. No matter how many goddamn times I fuck her, she still belongs to that fucking rat-bastard MC. But I can't summon up the rage when I look at her.

I slide my arm from her and tear my gaze away as I walk out of the bedroom.

"I don't know what the hell you are."

* * *

"So you decided to get married—just like that?"

Detective Asshat is not buying our bullshit. He leans over the table with his suspenders and his wire-rimmed glasses, looking too fucking serious for his own job.

Beatrice sits in my lap, positively glowing as I wrap my arms around her waist and give her a kiss on the side of her head.

"Yeah. True love knows no bounds, and all that shit."

Her nails dig into my neck.

"Excuse me?"

The other one, Detective Fatass, slams his meaty fist on the table, making Beatrice gasp.

"Stop fucking around, you piece of shit. We know you were at the Trudeau airport, along with Johnny Cravotta and his crew."

"I'd appreciate it if you stopped scaring my wife."

Beatrice turns her head to look straight at Detective Fatass. "He was with me that night."

"What were you doing for five hours?"

"Fucking."

Beatrice sends me an appropriately scandalized look, which I wave off.

"For five hours?"

"You sound surprised. Is your stamina not up to snuff?"

Fattass's face deepens to an ugly puce color. "You're telling me that you were having sexual intercourse with this woman for five hours straight?"

"I took a few fifteen minute breaks because her pussy was getting sore."

The look of pure rage might not be entirely feigned on her part.

I smile right in the face of those jerk-offs.

"We've given our statements. Can we go now?"

Her nails dig hard into my skin and I smooth my hand over her belly, giving her a small pinch.

Yeah, see how you like it.

"Yes."

The two detectives look like they've been denied a great treat, and Beatrice slides off my lap. She walks away from me and gives me a look filled with poison behind the two cops' backs.

"I'd say it's been a pleasure, but it hasn't."

I sweep past the two cops and palm open the door. Well, that was easy, wasn't it? A bubble of unease swells inside my stomach. Sure, I got off lucky, but that doesn't mean I'm off their radar. One screwup and they'll find a reason to make an arrest. It only takes one filthy rat to bury me, and the MC is full of them.

I wrap my arm around Beatrice's small waist, hating how my

blood pounds when she stops in the middle of the hallway and turns in my arms with a scorching gaze. She grabs the scruff of my neck and brings me closer, wearing a cute smile. Her lips crush mine as she pushes my back into the wall. Heat floods my veins as her tongue flicks inside my mouth, teasing me.

What the fuck is she doing?

We're in the middle of the police station, and she's shoving her tongue down my throat. Not that I mind, but it's a little weird even for me.

But I stop worrying about that when I feel her curves pressing into my body. God, I want her. I kiss her back, my arms wrapped around her because I want to touch every inch of what belongs to me. Beatrice pulls away, smiling, her eyes heavily lidded.

"I love you, baby."

She makes a trail with her fingers up my chest as I recover from what feels like a heavy book thrown in my face. Has she lost her mind?

"Uh—*what?*"

A triumphant snort from a man brushing past us in the hall averts my attention. Detective Fatass sneers at me with a side glance, and I turn back to Beatrice, her smile strained.

"I love you, too. Let's go."

Nothing ever sounded so forced. Beatrice cringes at my tone, her eyebrows narrowing before she gives a bizarre laugh and kisses my cheek.

I grab her upper arm and lead her down the hall, and it's only once until we're outside and well out of sight that she rounds on me, shoving my chest.

"What the hell is wrong with you?"

I don't like the way she looks at me. I take a step back and brush my jacket, pretending to be cool when I feel hot.

"You're going to have to be more specific."

"You're treating this like a fucking joke. 'Love knows no bounds, and all that shit'? Are you crazy?"

"Give me a break. They already know we're full of it."

She rolls her eyes. "After that performance, yeah."

"What, am I supposed to fawn over you like some lovesick moron?"

Her stony gaze meets mine, and I feel a ripple of anger from the contempt burning in her eyes.

"Do you *want* to go to jail?"

I don't have time for this. "Get in the fucking car."

The car door swings open in my hand and I watch her duck her head as she slides into the passenger seat. I slam the door shut and the car trembles with the force. My hands clench over the edge of the hood and the window as rage boils my insides.

Calm the fuck down.

I get into my car and we drive out of there in complete silence. I'm afraid of the mood I'm in. Lately I've been in towering rages only tempered by drugs and booze. Johnny made me quit the drugs, but I couldn't stop drinking. It's the only thing that helps.

I roll up to the curb in front of my house, but I don't cut the engine.

"I'm going out. I'll be back later."

Blue eyes cut at me as she turns her head and presses her lips together. Beatrice knows that I have a week off work. There's a splinter of pain in her eyes that almost immediately glosses over into what she tries to pass off as indifference.

"Whatever."

Yeah, whatever.

* * *

The drinks keep coming, and I slam them down like I'm dying of thirst. It'll take a few hours before I'm okay to drive home, but I'm fine with that. Anything to avoid being in the same room with my wife. The wife I keep fantasizing about: her naked curves in my hands, the way her pussy wraps around my dick, her lips, her tits—everything. I'm not supposed to want her; I'm supposed to hate her.

A hand slaps down on my shoulder. "How's the marriage?"

Johnny slides on the stool next to me, and I choke down my bitterness.

He's the boss. He's the boss.

"Pretty shitty so far."

His hand casually grips the back of my neck, and he gives me that fake smile that always precludes pain.

"Come with me. I want to talk to you."

I slide off the stool and follow John's strong grip into the back rooms of Tommy's bar. He drops the smile the moment we're alone.

"What the *fuck* are you doing in this bar?"

"I can't have a drink without your permission?"

He grits his teeth. "You're supposed to be spending this time with your new wife. That's why I gave you a week off."

Why don't you fucking lay off me, you prick?

"Ignoring her like this the day after your wedding is an insult to the MC—and an insult to me."

Violent images stream through my brain, interrupting the voices screaming at me. Do not piss off John. He'll get rid of you, just like he got rid of your brother.

"I need this marriage to work. You will *not* screw this up and cost me this alliance."

"You spit on the memory of my brother, and I'm supposed to be grateful?"

Fuck you.

Johnny's irate face swims closer. "You better be really fucking careful how you talk to me, or you're going to wind up just like him."

"Jack!"

A familiar voice barks at me. Recognizing Sal is the only thing that stops me from lunging at Johnny's throat. Thankfully the asshole turns around and walks out of the back room.

"Come here, damn it."

Sal is a beefy guy with a round, honest face. His dark-blue blazer hangs over his belly, and he pats the table where he's sitting, gesturing at me to sit down. He's a friendly guy, but he's still the underboss. Just one rank removed from boss.

"Sit down, Jack."

I'm still pissed off, but he gives me a look that's enough to shut down my smart mouth. Heaving a sigh, I pull back the chair and sit my ass down.

He reaches across the table, concern knitting his face as he grabs my hand. Usually I don't like being touched. When my brother died, every pat on the back felt fake. I look at these people—these men who are supposed to be my brothers—and I wonder which one of them did it, if the family was responsible. Which one killed him?

"I'm worried about you."

A smile tugs at my mouth. "Is that right?"

"The way you talk to the boss is going to get you clipped."

I know that. I'm probably one more fucking sentence from getting a bullet to the back of my head.

"I can't fucking do it anymore. I can't pretend like my brother isn't dead."

"No one's forgotten."

"*He* has. That son of a *bitch.* You know damn well he had something to do with it."

Sal gives me a warning look. "Watch your fucking mouth."

"You know I'm right."

"*I don't.* He was worried your brother would flip, but he would never do anything like that without proof."

Lead settles into my guts and I ball my fist under Sal's hand.

Oh Jesus Christ.

He did it, didn't he? It's confirmation for me. He did it. He was afraid my brother would talk. What about what the nurse said? A man in a suit. Thin face. Someone from the mob commissioned this hit, but I can't find a shred of fucking proof. The man at the top makes all the decisions. It's him.

That sick, helpless feeling consumes me again. How the fuck am I supposed to kill a boss? I'll be honest. Things like this happen to people's families. Guys fuck up. They get killed. It happens all the time and we're just supposed to swallow down our pride and accept it.

I can't accept it.

"Jack, I know that look on your face."

I pull my hand away from his, my brother's loss hitting me hard like a knife to my gut.

"When both of our parents died, he was the one who raised me. I was eight and he was a teenager."

"Yeah, you've told me."

"He dropped out of school to take care of me."

It's odd how little I remember of my parents. It was just Mike for a long time.

Memories of my older brother cycle through my head. He was always so goddamn tall. I see him in slacks and suspenders, rolling up a paper bag lunch. He hands the bag to me with a wink. "Here, kid. Learn something."

My chest feels like it's caving in. I miss him. He was always the faster one, the smarter one, even when we were both adults. Mike was better than me with a gun, got more girls than I did, and everyone loved him. He was more than just a brother or father. He was a god. I worshipped him.

Seeing him like that on the hospital bed, his spirit completely broken, was like watching him die. There was no twinkle in his eyes—no wisecrack—just listlessness. Waiting for death.

Fuck.

"I know you loved your brother, but you're no good to him dead."

Sal's fucking right.

"I know, but what am I supposed to do?" I hate how my voice cracks. "What would Mike do?"

Then his voice drops to a low growl. "Mike would have bided his time until the opportunity came to hit back at those assholes."

"You don't think this is going to last, do you? This alliance?"

"Somebody's going to talk. Johnny can't get to all the witnesses."

Fuck.

"Sooner rather than later."

"And then?"

"Then you go to jail when your wife rats you out, and we're back to where we fucking started, at war with the Devils MC while this investigation kills this family."

A cold feeling spreads down my limbs. How long would it take Johnny to decide to get rid of me while I'm in prison? I have no more leads to follow now that I've whacked the nurse. I can't very well start interrogating people in our crew.

"What am I supposed to do?"

Sal talks in a voice low enough so that I have to strain my ears to listen.

"Get on his good side. There's a job Johnny wants done by the end of the week. If you want to do it, let me know."

"All right. Send me the details."

The chair scrapes back as I stand up from the table. Fuck, my nerves are all jangled from this. I hate feeling jumpy, but if Sal's right then I have to be proactive. I walk to his side and bend over, embracing him.

"Thanks, Sal. I don't know what I'd do without you looking out for me."

He pats me on the back. "I can't help you if you don't help yourself, Jack."

"No, trust me. I'm on it."

I should have never let myself go like this. There's too much at stake, and I don't want to die. My brother's dead, but that doesn't mean I have to join him. Not when there's a chance to get back at the people who destroyed him.

The car's engine vibrates beneath my feet as I drive back to my place, everything that Sal said running through my brain like fire. I'm still untangling all the strings.

Bide your time.

Until what?

Until you can make a move on John, or the bikers, or both.

I listen to that steely voice inside me. Sal all but confirmed that John was the one behind his murder. And what if he's right? Someone will talk and the alliance will crumble, and I'll have this wife as a fucking liability that no one will trust.

Fuck the girl. Make her yours. Take her from them.

Yes.

Make her part of your family.

The list of my family is pretty fucking small. It's just me, aside from a handful of aunts and uncles on my mother's side who I've never met.

The voice inside me laughs.

I can't figure it out, and blood churns through my head as I drive home. Like it or not, that biker wife of mine is my ticket back into Johnny's good graces.

I'm after revenge. It's time to be smart about it, and that means making nice with the girl, bringing her along to all of the family events, and showing everyone else that I can make my biker wife toe the line.

As I roll up to my place I see something that's like a gunshot to my chest. Something that burns inside me like acid.

A man wearing a leather cut jacket. He's standing at my door, peering inside the window.

All of a sudden the sound turns off. I see myself cut the engine and the car door flies open. I pounce on him before the bastard can turn around. My hand grabs the back of his neck and I yank. He falls, tripping over the stairs. His body sails over them until he reaches the landing and then his head cracks over the pavement.

Cool rage controls my movements. I lift up my foot and slam it into his chest. I feel the crunch of his bones underneath my feet.

Again and *again.* His beardless face twists with moans that I can only barely hear. He flails like an ugly insect on the ground.

Then a soft touch curls around my arm, and the sound finally returns. It's a feminine voice, screaming in my ear. "STOP!"

I ignore her and bend over the piece of shit moaning at my feet. "Come to my house? You show up at my *fucking* doorstep?"

My boot lashes out, connecting with the side of his ribs. He flips over and I see the white embroidery: DEVILS MC.

"Jack, stop!"

He moans. "I just wanted—"

"You just wanted to what?"

I bend down and grab a handful of his brown hair, and I wrench him to a sitting position.

"I wanted to visit Beatrice."

I lower my face to his until he flinches from my closeness. "Stay the fuck away from my wife, or I'll kill you."

"I wasn't trying—"

"Get the fuck out of here!"

Then I release his greasy head and turn around, burning with rage as I grab Beatrice's arm and drag her up the steps.

"What the hell did you do?"

I throw her inside the apartment. She jumps when I slam the door.

"Who the fuck was that?"

Big blue eyes widen at me as she tugs the hem of her skirt down. The sight of long, creamy thighs distracts me for a moment.

"Paul—he was just—he wanted to see if I was okay." Her eyes fill with tears. "You didn't have to hurt him."

I take another step forward, noticing that she has her hair piled up on her head. Delicate blonde wisps frame her face. It only makes her look even more fragile.

"I told you that I didn't want to see them at my house. Ever."

"They're my family."

"Your family destroyed mine. He was all I had, don't you fucking understand that?"

My hand throbs from the beating I gave that piece of shit. Fear shines from her wide eyes. She looks as though I fucking hit her. I take a step closer and I grab the back of her delicate neck, inhaling the spicy scent of ginger.

"It's not fair," she breathes, her eyes squeezed shut.

I feel her breaking under my hands, shaking like a delicate bird. My fingers sweep under her chin.

"Look at me."

She obeys. I stare into her liquid blue eyes, tiny droplets clinging on her blonde eyelashes.

"I hate to break it to you, but life's not fair."

"You shouldn't punish me for this—I had nothing to do with the people who killed him."

"You're complicit. You're one of them."

"They don't care about me!"

Something inside me breaks as her eyes well up with tears and they suddenly spill over her cheeks.

"My dad never wanted me to do this. I should have listened."

There's a freckle on her upper lip. Blood pounds through my cock. She shakes her head.

"Maybe you should have."

Her mouth twists into a savage snarl and she shoves my chest. "I hate you!"

I grab her flailing arm and drag her into the bedroom, where there's a full-length mirror. I reach up into her head of hair and dig my fingers in as confusion shivers over Beatrice's face. I watch myself, smirking, as I snake my arm around her waist to pin her to me.

"You can hate me all you want, sweetheart. God knows I love a good hate fuck."

Then I pull her hair a little bit so that she bends over my arm, and then I kiss her soft neck, all the way down to her clavicle.

"You hate me… You want me."

"I'm pretty sure I just hate you."

I watch my mouth spread into a smile as she squirms in my arms. "Yeah? Let's find out how wet you are just from being held by me."

I slide from her waist to hike up her skirt, enjoying the view of her upper thigh being exposed. Then I move my hand up her smooth skin, giving her ass a squeeze before I hook my fingers over her panties and pull them down her silky legs. They drop to her ankles and she presses her legs together.

"You broke the rules."

Her perky ass almost demands a slap, and I quickly spank her left cheek.

"Spread your legs, or you'll get another one."

Breathing hard, she moves her legs an inch apart, and my finger glides around her hip and up her gorgeous thighs to slip in her wetness. Her pussy is soaked for me. My cock grows inside my slacks as I watch her face collapse.

"Yeah, I think you're a little liar."

She looks so fucking hot with my hand up her skirt, her breasts heaving as she grabs the arm as if to throw it off, but she can't go through with it.

"Why—why are you doing this?"

Revenge. Fuck the MC. I'll take one of your daughters and turn her into my dick-sucking slave. I'll make her worship me. She'll be mine.

"'Cause I want you."

I fuck her pussy, digging my fingers deep into her wet cunt as I tear off her shirt, and the sight of her topless makes my dick jump. I press her against the glass as she moans.

"I want you to look at yourself. Look how turned-on you are."

My fingers thrust hard between her legs, and she lets out a cry. "Jack!"

"Look at yourself."

She turns her head and looks, seeing her panting expression and me behind her. My hand squeezes each of her round tits and then I play with her hard nipples, twisting them with my fingers. She moans hard.

Jesus Christ, I want to sink my cock into her.

I've almost had enough of her bucking against my hand, but then she turns her head and kisses me like she's never kissed me before. It's fucking rough and full of teeth.

My other hand slips out between her legs and I bring it to her face. She pulls away from me, her lips swollen as I move the finger covered in her juices over her mouth. Her tongue teases my fingers as she sucks every last drop.

Then my fingers fall from her mouth and she gives me a plaintive look.

I feel her ass riding against my stiff cock, and more than anything I want to watch myself bang her in front of this mirror.

With a few swift jerks my slacks fall to the floor, and Beatrice shudders as she feels my length against her back.

"I want you to watch yourself as I bury my cock in you."

And then I tug down my briefs, hissing as the cool air hits my shaft. I pull a condom from the nightstand and rip it open, rolling it over me. Then I pull her lips apart, guiding my cock into her wet heat.

She gives such a high gasp that I'm sure I hurt her, until she collapses against the mirror.

Oh God, the fucking relief. It washes over me the moment I sink into her and ram my cock home. All the bullshit in my life fades away, and I only care about giving her my cum.

"Hands against the mirror."

Beatrice spreads her legs wide and places her hands on the mirror, bending over to give me a nice view of her ass. I flip the skirt over her back and watch her face contort with pleasure and pain.

Fuck, she feels good. Her cunt is like smooth silk over my cock, warm and welcoming. It opens up, letting me in deeper, until my balls crush against her pussy and she lets out a sharp moan. The rhythmic slapping gets my blood boiling, the feeling of her hips in my hands, and even seeing myself pounding this bitch.

I spank her ass once, twice, watching blood rise to the surface of her skin. I watch it move in tandem with my fucking. She balls her fists on the mirror and cries out.

"More, Jack!"

I reach forward and grab a ponytail of hair. I yank back, forcing her to arch.

"Shut up and take my cum."

The friction gets intense, and I feel my balls heating up. Close. So close. Loud smacks fill the room as I fuck her harder. She's screaming so loud that we're going to get the cops called on us.

I wrap my arm around her waist and I swing her upright, crushing her against the glass as I drive into her. My other hand still yanks her hair, and I dig my fingers deep. I find her pussy and I press down over her clit, and her moans deepen.

"Holy shit, Jack!"

Then I feel it ripping through me. Her muscles tighten around my cock and I thrust hard, releasing my cum into her. I have to keep fucking her. Everything inside me wants that cum shoved as deep as possible, but of course the condom catches it all. Her pussy contracts beneath my fingers as I pulse in and out, the wave of pleasure receding.

I slip out of her and she turns around, wrapping her arms around my neck and digging her fingers into my hair. It feels amazing.

She lifts herself on her toes to kiss me, and incredible warmth fills my chest. Then I wonder if she's becoming mine or if I'm becoming hers.

BEATRICE

My eyes feel like sandpaper and my head pounds. I run my finger along the sharp edge of the blade, and I think about what my dad wanted me to do. There's a way out, if I had the courage to do it.

Slit his throat while he sleeps.

A visceral, gut-wrenching feeling makes me drop the knife. No. Jack might be a bastard, but he doesn't deserve to die. I'm the one who deserves to be punished. I'm the one carrying this big, awful secret around. His brother's death eats him alive. I see it every day, when he buries himself in drinks. I still haven't said a word.

I stand up from the couch, staring at all the boxes, and I walk aimlessly to another room. All I know is that it's been a week into our marriage, and I'm losing my damn mind.

He beat the shit out of Paul just for showing up at my doorstep.

I bend down and pick up the knife that I know I won't use.

My stomach roils with it. He's completely the opposite of me—a maniac who flies off the handle. I'm a mouse by comparison.

Grabbing my purse, I decide to go out for a walk. As I stroll into the brilliant rays of sunshine, unease settles in my stomach. I'm not used to this Italian neighborhood yet. I feel like an intruder even though I'm married to one of them.

I sling my purse over my shoulder and fighting the tinge of nausea when I see three guys loitering on the sidewalk, smoking. The way they won't stop staring at me gives me a really bad feeling. They look older and very rough around the edges. Degenerates. My insides clench and I look down as I pass them.

"*Ey, pitoune*!"

"How are you, sweetie? *Hey*!"

Fuck.

I walk right between them, keeping my head down as I head straight for the corner store. The glass doors slide and I stumble gratefully into the air-conditioned grocery. I grab a basket and fill it with a few things and then I notice the voices speaking at the register in melodic Italian. I'm just getting a couple things for dinner, and as I weave through the aisles I listen to them talking. It's so much prettier than French.

There's a man in dark jeans leaning over the counter at the register. He sees me approach and leans back, digging a cigarette out of his pocket. The girl behind the counter gives him a secretive smile and turns to me.

"*Si, prego.*"

"Oh—I don't speak Italian."

She nods and rings me up. I pay her with a hundred-dollar bill and take the change from her blindly. The man makes a remark in Italian and the girl laughs. The harsh sound hits my ears and I grab the plastic bag.

I get out of there, the sunlight doing nothing to lift my spirits, and those guys are still there. They whistle at me as soon as I exit the store.

God fucking damn it.

"Hey, why you don't like us?"

"*C'est quoi ton problème?*"

Just don't look at them. Ignore.

"*Vache.*"

The insult hits me right in the face and tears spring to my eyes as I walk away furiously. It's not until I'm several blocks away that I realize that the cashier gave me the wrong change. She shorted me by about forty bucks.

Jesus.

I look back, but the guys are still there. The idea of walking through them again and confronting the girl makes me want to vomit, so I keep going. Even though I hate myself for it.

God, how pathetic am I?

When I get home, I put the money and the groceries next to each other on the kitchen table so that I can feel shitty about myself the whole day. I'm listless around the apartment. I consider cleaning up a little, but he told me not to touch his things.

Hours later I hear the scrape of a key and a lock being turned, and I'm almost happy to see Jack stumble in the apartment.

"Hey," he says in a low voice.

He walks into the living room and sinks into the couch beside me with a sharp sigh, and then I look at his face. There's a huge, ugly red mark on the side of his face, and his hands are cracked with dry blood.

"Oh my God, what happened?"

"Ran into a little trouble."

I stand up abruptly, heading straight for the freezer where I dig out a bag of frozen peas. He slips out of his shoes and throws his jacket on a nearby chair as if everything's normal.

"What the hell happened?"

"Don't worry about it."

I sit back down next to him, feeling strangely diminished beside him, and then I hold the bag of peas to his face.

Jack hisses slightly as the cold comes in contact with his raw wounds, and then a slow sigh leaves his mouth.

"That looks really bad," I say in a high voice.

He frowns and makes a dismissive gesture with his hand. "Will you stop with the dramatics? Johnny needed something done."

I try to figure out why Jack's wounds bother me so much, and then it hits me.

I'm nothing without him.

The MC won't let me back in, and Johnny sure as shit won't take care of me. He's all I've got.

Oh fuck.

"What's the matter with you?"

My mood blackens and I feel my chest tightening as though my body is trying to suffocate itself. He puts his hand over the one holding the frozen peas to his face. The pressure in my head is about to explode, and the soft voice Jack uses makes it even worse.

"Nothing," I say in a thick voice.

I slide my hand out from under his and then I stand up, walking slowly to the kitchen. Breathe. Calm down. I take a seat at the table, out of his sight, but those crumpled bills sit right in the middle, staring me in the face.

And I blubber like a fucking baby.

I clamp my hands over my mouth to stifle the noise, but it's too late. The scrape of Jack's feet alerts me to his presence.

"Look," he begins in a softer voice. "You're going to have to get used to seeing me hurt. I can't come home to you crying like this."

"You don't understand."

His face loosens and he takes another few steps forward. His hand lies heavily on my shoulder. "I don't understand how a girl who grew up in the MC could get like this. I thought you'd be tougher."

I'm not tough at all.

"It's been a really bad day."

I want to smack the smirk from his face. He tries to sober his expression and touches my arm.

I wrench it away from him. "Could you just leave me alone?"

I don't look at his face. I only see the hand clenched at his side and his wavering legs. He hesitates, clenching and unclenching his hand. Then he pulls out a chair and sits down next to me, touching my hair and face. It almost feels sweet.

"Just tell me, Beatrice."

Oh God.

I wipe my face and stare at the kitchen table. "I just—I was stiffed at the grocery store down the block."

"You were *what*?"

He grabs my shoulder and leans in, all amusement gone from his face.

"They shorted me about forty dollars."

"So why the hell didn't you go back to complain?"

Shame creeps in from the frustration in his voice. I think of the three guys harassing me on the street and my paralyzing fear preventing me from marching right through them.

"There were a few guys on the corner giving me a hard time." I bite my tongue from revealing any more. The last thing I want is him flying off the handle because some dumbass on the street corner called me a cow.

His voice hardens. "What did they say?"

"*Nothing*."

"Don't lie to me, Beatrice."

"They were hitting on me and being assholes about it."

The bag of peas hits the table with a hard thump and Jack stands up from the chair, grabbing my hand. I follow the pressure, anxiety leaping inside me when I see the darkness on his face.

"Come on."

The keys scrape across the wood as he grabs them from the table and nearly yanks me down the hall. I dig my heels in and he whirls around.

"Wait— What are you doing?"

"Going to the fucking grocery store to break some goddamn heads."

Oh my God.

"Jack!"

He bends down swiftly, taking my head in his hands as his

demeanor shifts suddenly. A sweet smile staggers across his face before he kisses me twice on my lips. Heat pricks across my chest as he pulls back.

"I'm not going to just give a pass to people who fuck over my wife."

"Promise me you won't hurt anyone."

Shock makes his face blank for a moment and then the smile returns. "I won't. I promise."

I feel strong walking by Jack's side, his hand firmly clasped around mine. He doesn't say much as we walk down the street, but I can see the fury building up behind his eyes. The three men at the corner are nowhere in sight, but that doesn't stop Jack from looking down all the streets for them.

"Cocksuckers."

He opens the door to the grocery store for me and I walk inside, noticing that the same cashier is working. There's only one other customer inside. Jack enters the store smoothly, scanning it before sliding up to the customer browsing the frozen food section. He taps him on his shoulder and the customer turns to face him, confused.

Jack only has to utter a few words. "Take a walk."

The man does a double take and drops his basket of groceries on the floor.

"Sorry," he mutters unnecessarily.

My heart skips ahead as Jack follows him and flips the sign on the door to CLOSED. Head pounding, I try to mouth him a question: *What are you doing?* He ignores me, joining me at my side. He takes my hand again, which slips in his, and he marches me to the counter.

Crap. What the hell is he planning?

The cashier perks her head up, noticing Jack, and gives him a much warmer smile than she gave me.

"Hello, Jack." Her sycophantic gaze slides over to me. "Who's this?"

"This is my wife, Beatrice. She tells me she ran into a bit of trouble at the store today."

Recognition slowly dawns over her face and she quickly covers her mouth to hide a gasp. My fingers slip as he approaches the counter and stares her down.

"What kind of trouble?"

"Don't play dumb, or I'm going to get pissed."

She pushes herself from the counter and blinks rapidly, wrapping her arms around herself. "I—I don't know what she's talking about."

A loud crash makes her jump and scream. Jack slams his fist into the cash register, making it fly open. He reaches over and grabs handfuls of bills, cleaning out half the goddamn thing. A lump rises in my throat as he slowly stuffs the bills in his pocket. She flinches as he reaches over again and slams the register closed.

"What the hell are you doing?"

"You shorted my wife forty bucks, you dumb bitch!"

The cashier gives me a cutting glare. "It was an accident!"

Jack leans back with a strained smile. "Ah, an accident. I see."

He's like a tiger. Suddenly he pounces to the right and grabs something that swings with a wide arc. Glass cracks as he whales against the upright case of drinks. He throws his body into swinging the bat into the glass case. Hundreds of jagged pieces of glass shatter and fall to his feet, spilling cold air into the store.

"What the fuck are you doing? Stop it!"

"What?" he says, raising his arms, still holding the bat. "It was an accident!"

Oh my God, what a psycho!

The girl backs away, her eyes as big as saucers as she hits the wall.

Goddamn it.

"Jack, stop!"

I move between him and the register, shoving his chest. He gives me a look of feigned surprise.

"What? My hand slipped!"

Jesus Christ. He's a fucking lunatic.

The cashier pipes up in a small voice, "I'm sorry, all right? I—I didn't know who she was."

He waves the bat in her face. "The next time you take advantage of my wife, I'll shove this bat up your ass."

Then he lets it fall, and it clangs on the floor next to the broken glass. He curls an arm around my waist and jerks me to his side, his fingers spreading warmth through my body. My ribs seem to jump against my t-shirt as he walks me across the grocery store, opening the door to let me out. I flinch when he returns to my side.

"What the hell is wrong with you?"

"You," I say in a shaking voice. "You're a lunatic."

I can't believe I signed up for a lifetime of *this*. Growing up I never saw an ounce of violence. Sure, the guys would get a little too drunk every so often and things would get out of hand, but nothing that made me sick with fear.

"Why?"

I pull away from him and study his swollen face, and I think about how I really never had a goddamn clue about the lives the members in the MC led.

"You just trashed her store and stole half her money for no reason."

"I have a reputation to maintain on the streets, sweetheart."

"What, that you fly off the handle at every slight?"

He lets out a gale of laughter. "You act like you didn't grow up in the MC."

Maybe it's the sight of his battered face that has my heart racing. Without him, I have nowhere to go.

So I say nothing.

My face burns as I stare at the street, and we walk in silence all the way back to his house. He slides his arms around my waist the moment we're alone. I freeze in as the image of him swinging the bat burns in my mind. I hate the way my skin pricks with heat the moment I feel his hands on me. I'm supposed to tame him, and I'm doing a pretty shitty job of it so far. He turns me around so that we're facing each other and then gently backs me against a wall, sliding a thigh between my legs.

Holy crap.

The hardness of his thigh rides my pussy and for a moment all I can think about is how amazing he always makes me feel.

"Jack, you're risking your life," I whisper when he bends his head. "It's way too reckless."

"That wasn't a risk. The people in this neighborhood know who I am."

Didn't work out so well for your brother, did it? Then I feel a stab of shame at that thought, because every time I think of his brother I feel a fresh wave of hot, bubbling guilt.

"One of these days, Beatrice, you're going to have to stand up for yourself."

"Like you?" I quip before I can stop myself.

He thumbs my mouth as his eyes fuck me. Then a smirk pulls at his lips. "Maybe."

My stomach shivers as he flattens his hand and moves down my waist, parting the waistband of my jeans to curve over my mound and gently stroke my throbbing nub. He laughs in my mouth, centimeters from a kiss. The air billowing over my lips makes my heart jackknife into my chest.

"No panties. That must be really uncomfortable."

Yes, it is, you crazy asshole.

A wet heat slides across my lips, and then he presses his whole body against me. His mouth descends over mine and my cheeks flame as desire makes my flesh ache. Then he slips his hand out of my pants. His body disappears from my side and he walks away from me, throwing a grin over his shoulder as he enters the kitchen and grabs a tall, skinny bottle.

Fucking bastard.

My head pounds as he sits down at the kitchen table and pours himself a drink. "We're going to a party downtown tonight. Johnny will expect you to be there."

I exhale a huge breath and walk closer to him, pulling out a chair to sit next to him.

"Are you going to be a good girl and behave, or am I going to have to bend you over my knee?"

"I don't like him, Jack." A cold feeling spreads through my limbs whenever I think about his lifeless stare.

"Your cousin will be there."

Maya?

I fidget in my chair with an excited squirm. "And the baby?"

He gives me a strange look. "I don't know. Probably."

Happy thoughts of that beautiful baby burst as Jack pours himself a drink and inhales it. The table trembles as he slams it down. He shoots me an angry look. "*What*?"

I tentatively reach for his arm, but he pulls it away. "You look upset."

Jack's brows furrow as he violently grabs the glass, nearly spilling the bottle's contents on the table. He slams it back and swallows, screwing up his face.

"Is it your brother?"

"The fuck do you care?"

The sting hits my face, thrown by the contempt in his voice. I picture the moment his brother died in my mind. I was there. I want to tell him that I saw three men wearing leather cuts through the darkened window. The desire swells up inside me. I look at his face, slightly red with alcohol.

And I can't tell him.

The pain weighs down his shoulders. Fuck, I never thought I'd feel bad for one of them until I married him. My gut wrenches as I imagine it over and over—the pillow over his face and their smooth, indifferent expressions.

He raises the drink to his lips and throws his head back. Seething eyes cut me as he lets the glass drop on the table. It shudders in his hand when he swallows the drink.

I look around the apartment, trying to seize on something that will distract him. "Jack, why are there boxes everywhere?"

I noticed them the first time I stepped in his apartment. Did he just move in?

He shuts his eyes as if in pain. "They're Mike's stuff."

"Oh."

Good fucking job.

The guilt eats at my insides like a plague and I stand up to get away from it. It's not my problem. What the hell do I care about some dead Mafia asshole?

Jack buries his face in his hands, his elbows sitting on the table.

A dagger hits my chest.

"He was the only family I had," he says in a heavy voice.

He uncovers his face and that wound still throbs in a big, shining lump. I walk over to the discarded frozen peas. They're still cold. My footsteps echo hollowly as I return to the kitchen and grab a couple paper towels. I use the sink to wet them slightly and then I stand in front of him. My hand trembles with the towels as I place them over his face. He jerks his head to the side and pushes my waist.

"Stop."

"Let me help."

"I'm fine."

"No, you're not."

"I can deal with this. *Alone*."

"Well, you're not alone."

I sit down on his lap and he lets out a frustrated sigh as I raise the sodden paper towels to that nasty gash on his forehead. I blot it gently, the dried blood smearing over the towel.

I'm close enough to see the small flecks of emerald in his eyes. They slide over to me and hold my gaze, and I forget what I'm doing. I'm just caught in his heavy stare as my heart becomes suddenly aware of how close we are.

"Does it hurt?"

Jack doesn't respond. I just feel the slow burn creeping up my neck as his eyes refuse to let go of me. Flustered, I dry his face, gently patting, and then I hold the frozen peas against his head. Butterflies flutter in my stomach. I want to touch him—kiss him—but I'm afraid to. Despite being married to him, I don't feel like he's mine yet.

And I want that.

I desperately want that.

* * *

Silence.

The silence stretches thin, wavering like a solitary note on a piano key. The night whisks past my window. It feels weird to be inside the car. I'm so used to wrapping my arms around a broad back and just feeling the breeze freeing my hair.

The red mark still shines brightly on his head, but he doesn't look like he gives a shit. Even that horrible blemish isn't enough to dim Jack's radiance. A smooth black suit, like liquid ink, covers his body. He looks really good—a lot better than he deserves.

Jack eyes cut at me occasionally, almost narrowed in suspicion. I eye his hand resting on the gear, wishing I could lace his fingers through mine, wishing I had an ounce of his affection.

You don't deserve it.

"Hey, listen. Thanks for—uh, defending me at the grocery store."

I'll admit that a part of me felt a small amount of savage triumph. He was so passionate about protecting me that it almost felt real.

He shakes his head with a smile, saying nothing.

"Jack, do you think that the alliance will last?"

The smile disappears as though it was slapped off his face. He gives me a sharp glance and then stares straight ahead. "No."

"What do you mean, no?"

Panic suddenly flares up my spine as he shakes his head.

"It won't last. There are too many people willing to fold under pressure and rat the other side out." He doesn't need to add that he couldn't care less.

What will happen to us?

"What was the point of all this if it was just going to fall apart anyway?"

"Revenge. That's the fucking point."

The car lurches to a stop as he pulls up beside the street, and I realize with a start that we're already there. I look down at my lap and grab my knees as a wave of vertigo hits me.

"What does that mean?"

His hand suddenly curves around my thigh and he leans across the divide, nuzzling my ear. "I'm going to take the sweet, innocent girl they gave me and use her as my fuck-toy." His hand inches up my thigh and touches my wetness just briefly. "I'll use you until I'm too exhausted to hate them."

Then his fingers spread me open and I gasp as he enters me, hand curled under my dress. His mouth crushes against mine. I hear my wetness around his fingers, and the heat of his palm cupping my pussy sends electricity up my spine. My skin tingles as he roughly grabs one of my tits, the sensation of his thumb flicking over my nipple overwhelming me.

Jesus Christ. We're in a car. Right under a streetlight.

We break from the kiss and he utters a low growl in my hair, still fucking me with his hand. "You want to be a good wife, don't you?"

My dress rides up my thighs, his fingers diving in and out of me easily. My moan rips through the car, and Jack's seductive smile hangs in front of me. "I asked you a question."

"Yeah—yeah, whatever!"

"Not 'whatever.'" The hand fondling my tits suddenly grabs my jaw.

"I'm a good wife!"

"Yes, you are. You never, ever disobey me. It's almost like you were born to take orders from a man."

Say whatever the fuck you want. Just keep doing this to me.

"Please, don't stop!"

He forces his fingers through my tight walls. I clench around him and run my fingers over his thrusting hand. It feels amazing.

"You want to come?"

The pressure builds up with every tight thrust, and I grab his arm so that he pauses. His fingers brush against my clit and a jolt hits my heart.

"Can I?"

"*No.*"

The word crashes over my ears and I press my thighs together, trapping his hand.

"No? Why not?"

"Are you arguing with me?" The question comes out in a growl, but I hear his chuckle right before he snags the neckline of my dress and pulls it down, exposing a swell of flesh. He takes me in his mouth before I can answer, sucking my nipple and biting down over the sensitive ring.

I arch my back as I feel his tongue slowly flicking over my nipple, the cool air stinging me before his hot mouth sucks me. He pulls until it stings, until I feel the burn even after he pulls back and smiles at the red mark. Then he slides his hand out from between my thighs and pulls my dress over my knees.

Are you fucking kidding me?

"I love seeing you so worked up."

I look at his lap and it's as if he stuffed a pipe down his pants. I reach over and slide my hands over his cock, curling my fingers around him. A thrill hits my heart when I feel it twitch. He makes a sound at the back of his throat that makes me flush. Then he takes my hand away.

"Let's go."

"But—"

"I promise I'll fuck you really hard if you behave tonight."

I'll have to spend the whole night aching for him. What a prick.

He pulls away from me, a ghost of a smile playing on his lips as he leaves the car and walks around. I'm still taking heavy breaths when he opens my car door. Jack takes my hand and I stand up on shaky feet, desire still pounding between my legs. He opens the plain black door and an explosion of music hits my face.

Jack's arm is snug around my waist as he nods to the hostess. Inside is an expansive lounge where a live band plays. The tables are polished to a black shine and solitary candles in glasses look like fireflies. We walk down the steps and onto the floor, to a huge table where the whole family seems to be gathered. All of the men I recognize from the brief moments I'd catch them at the MC are seated at the table with their wives. They're glitzy and beautiful, their hair styled on their heads like royalty. I look down at my summer dress and picture myself with my flat-ironed hair, and I feel completely stupid. I spot Maya talking happily to another woman with curly hair, and I see Johnny at the head of the table.

My husband tugs me along, making a beeline straight for his boss.

"Jack! How are you?"

Johnny stands up and Jack breaks away from me for a moment to embrace him. An uneasy feeling creeps inside my stomach as the Cravotta Crime Family boss merely gives me a curt nod and a smile.

"Ladies, this is my wife, Beatrice."

He introduces me to every single person at the table, including a portly man who wrings my hand, and I've already forgotten their names by the time we get to Maya. She beams at me.

She wears a floor-length black gown with a plunging neckline and a dangling, brilliant necklace. Everyone is decked out to the nines, and I'm in this stupid summer dress. Good lord.

"Sit down!"

I take a seat next to Maya, and Jack squeezes in beside me.

"I'm so glad you're here," I say fervently. "I'm so completely out of my element."

She waves off my concern. "You're fine, Bea."

"Where's your little boy?"

"Oh—Johnny's ma is watching him."

"Oh." I deflate a little. Seeing Maya's baby would've definitely been the highlight of the evening.

"I'll show you pictures!"

I lean over her shoulder as she scrolls through dozens of baby photos, and I fight a rising tide of jealousy at her perfect family life. I touch the screen, marveling at those chubby cheeks and the dark tuft of hair.

"He's beautiful."

Maya smiles knowingly. "Thanks."

It's not fair.

Emptiness yawns inside me as I scroll through the photos. I feel her hand on my shoulder.

"Hey, you'll get your chance."

"With who? *Him*?"

I glance at my husband, who lounges back in his chair with a sour look on his face. He's not happy to be here with me. He's not happy, period. And I know exactly why. Guilt twists inside me like the sharp end of a corkscrew, digging deeper and taking root. I have to fucking tell him, or I'll hate myself forever, but I can't help but think about the future. What if we had a baby?

Then Jack turns his head and gives me a curious look, and my face burns hot like a lamp.

"If you ever need a babysitter, just ask."

Maya nods, beaming. "Of course."

"We already have a babysitter, *ma belle*." Johnny leans in the conversation with a dark smile.

"*Be nice.*"

"I am fucking being nice."

She shoots him a glare and then looks over my head. "What happened to your face?"

Jack shifts in his chair and smiles at her, the swelling on his cheek more pronounced. "Occupational hazard."

"You gotta watch yourself, Jackie-boy."

An uncharacteristically ugly look comes over Jack's face. "Yeah, well, our boy Ben didn't show up, so I had to handle it—"

"*Not now.*"

Jack sits back into his chair, looking frustrated.

A cool hand grasps my arm, and I turn toward Maya.

"So how's everything going? With him?"

Suddenly I'm happy there's a roar of background noise to disguise our conversation.

I'm basically his whore.

"Not great."

"It wasn't easy for me either, but I'm happy now."

She looks it.

"You don't regret it?"

"No. I had no future at the MC."

Call me crazy, but I didn't mind it so much. Everyone had a place at the MC. Here? I don't know what the fuck I am.

"Let's just have a good time tonight!"

I try to smile back at my cousin as she pours me a glass of wine, but there's a heaviness in my chest that won't lift. Those fucking baby photos. They're just a reminder of what I can't ever have. Who knows how many years it'll take before this investigation is over?

I down a large sip of wine and hope that it purges the baby thoughts from my head. He would be terrible to have kids with anyway. Wouldn't he?

Then Jack grabs my wrist and my attention turns to the waiter hovering over me with a pad. I take the menu.

"I'll have the spaghetti with homemade meatballs."

He nods and moves down the table.

Jack's heavy arm drapes over my shoulders. His hand curls over my bare skin and my heart jumps, pleasure flooding my veins. Rough fingers pinch me suddenly.

"Stop talking to her. The boss doesn't like it."

I look above the table to see Johnny regarding me with thinly disguised contempt. A mixture of fear and anger wrestle inside me, and I turn back to Jack.

This time my lips graze his ear. "Fuck the boss. Isn't that what you always say?"

It's the alcohol talking.

He laughs, showing off his teeth. "You're going to get me killed."

I don't care if that asshole has a problem with me talking to his wife. Maya's my cousin. I turn toward her, but Jack grabs my thigh under the table and squeezes.

A faint feeling similar to the rush of wine temporarily paralyzes my body. He inches his hand farther, his deep eyes staring at me like he gives a shit about nothing else.

"What are you doing?"

My whole body shivers as he leans in, brushing his lips against my neck. "Distracting you."

Distracting me?

My thoughts repeat his words as though they're a different

language.

His finger brushes my inner thigh. I take his hand and dig my fingernails into him, and he retreats, laughing softly in my ear.

"You'll have to come over sometime, get to know the baby."

My attention turns back to my cousin as a confusing rush of emotions burns my face. "Yeah—of course! I'd love that."

Johnny wouldn't.

A huge plate of spaghetti and homemade meatballs is dropped in front of me. I wait until everyone has their food and then I pick up my knife and fork and I slice the pasta noodles.

"*What-the-fuck-are-you-doing?*"

I pause midway in between cutting the noodles, startled by the heat in Jack's voice. He gives me a look that's filled with poison.

"What's your problem?"

"Who the fuck taught you how to eat? You don't cut pasta!"

Jesus. From the way he sounds, it's as if I started eating with my hands.

He takes the knife out of my grip and sets it down. Then he takes my other hand with the fork and twists it in my fingers so that the prongs rest on the plate.

"You *spin* it."

"But I need a spoon."

He shuts his eyes as though I wounded him and even Johnny gives off a bark of laughter.

"No spoon, for fuck's sake."

A hot rush of shame floods my cheeks as a few of the others

chime in. I try to take it in stride, but I just feel so fucking down.

I don't belong here. I'm not one of them, and it's not just because of this. The way they look at me—with sneering contemptuous faces. Only Maya talks to me, but none of them would treat the boss's wife with disrespect. She's married to him. Has a kid with him. Of course she's one of them. There's no doubt, when clearly there's doubt with me.

Suddenly I remember Maya's healthy baby at her breast. A rush of longing hits me in the stomach so that even though I just ate, I feel empty.

The jazz band picks up a slow ballad, and Maya rises from her table, whispering in Johnny's ear. He smiles and stands up, too.

"Beatrice and I used to sneak out dancing whenever we could," she tells her husband, who gives me a small smile.

Feeling the urge to get away from the table, I stand up. "Jack, are you coming?"

He can't say no in front of everyone without looking like an utter ass. A warm smile that I've never seen on Jack unexpectedly sends a flight of butterflies.

"Of course."

I'm taken aback as he stands up and takes my waist, his mouth brushing my ear as though he means to kiss me. "I hate dancing."

Too fucking bad.

I follow Maya and Johnny to the dance floor, where they join hands and immediately look lost in each other. Jack spins me around and takes my hand. Goose bumps sprout over my arms as the fingers at my waist pull me in closer. It's hard not to feel utterly breathless when I'm in his arms.

"Are you happy? We're dancing."

"Yes, I am."

I love the smile that spreads across his face. I wish I could see it more often.

Maya gives us a little wave and I grin back at her. When I turn back to Jack, he's wearing a shrewd grin.

"Doesn't a part of you hate her for what she did?"

"Why would I hate her?"

"You wouldn't be here. Everyone who died would still be alive."

His eyes blaze suddenly and I know he's thinking of his brother.

"Jack, at the end of the day, all she was trying to do was be with him."

He shakes his head, still smiling. "You're a romantic. I'm not."

All he sees is the wave of devastation left behind.

"I don't know if I'd go back, even if I could."

"What?"

I bite my lip viciously as a lump grows in my throat. "Jett told me I couldn't come back. He made a threat."

"Wait, *what*? What do you mean, a threat?"

"He said Maya was dead to him and if I wasn't careful, I'd join her. All because I didn't stop them from meeting up."

It's so unfair.

Pain swells in my throat and I blink rapidly as Jack's mouth hangs open.

"I didn't know."

Then he holds me tightly so that our bodies mold together, and the warmth in my chest washes over the pain. The song ends and suddenly his fingers find my chin and he lays a soft kiss on my mouth. Heat rushes to my face as he dips me in his arms.

Holy shit!

I pretty much forget everything else once his wicked tongue does a dance inside my mouth. I cling to his neck as desire fans out in flames, and then he pulls me back upright, his hands making my heart flutter.

My skin tingles when he breaks away from me, and I look at his wet lips and want more.

"What was that?"

"That was to cheer you up."

He pulls back even farther and gives me a wink that makes the tips of my toes curl.

Jack hangs out with the guys for the rest of the night, and I slip away with Maya to the bar. Alcohol burns my tongue as three men I recognize from our table belly up.

"Hey, I'm going to the bathroom. Want to come?"

"No, I'll stay here."

Maya nods and walks off to the bathroom as I sit there, alone. The noise barely filters through my head, but then I catch two words that snap my attention.

"Fuck them. Sal was right, allying with those bastards was a mistake."

"We should have sent a message to the other crews."

A low, somber voice speaks up. "We did, remember?"

"One fucking dead biker isn't enough—"

"Yeah, well, if John hadn't fucked the president's daughter—"

"What do you think about Jack marrying that club whore?"

My heart pounds against my chest, and I turn in my seat, hoping like hell that they won't see my face.

"I would smack that cunt around and put her in her place."

"It's a fucking embarrassment, one of our guys marrying a club whore."

I can't take it anymore. My throat is thick with tears as I get off the stool and practically run toward the bathroom.

And I collide with a man's chest.

"Whoa!"

"I'm sorry," I say to his feet, stepping around him.

The feet step in front of me again. Then I want to charge past, because I just want to get to the bathroom and lose it. Someone grabs my arms.

"Hey, what's the matter?"

I tremble at the sound of his voice and look up into Jack's softened face.

"I want to leave. *Now.*"

His hands cradle my face and warmth blazes through his fingers, soothing my head. "What happened?"

"Something I ate. I don't feel good."

His hands fall from my face. "Well, that's complete bullshit, but

I'll take any excuse to get the fuck out of here."

He takes my hand and I nearly drag my heels on the way back to the table.

Club whore.

Cunt.

I'm still shaking when we walk out of that place. Jack gives me peculiar looks as we drive back to the city.

"Are you going to tell me what's made you so upset, or what?"

I bite my knuckle hard as he shakes his head and continues driving.

It's not until we're safely shut inside his apartment that I steel myself to say something. He hangs his coat and thrusts it in the closet, and then he turns around, finding me staring at him.

So much of what I heard from those guys sounded like it could've come from Jack's mouth.

"Do you hate me?"

He runs a hand through his hair, pained. Blood rushes to my face when he stops inches from my body. His eyes are like dark jewels, glowing hot. He reaches out and touches the bare skin right above the swell of my breast, where my heart beats like crazy. I smell the notes wafting from his skin—all masculine and aquatic. Every sound is magnified as he curls his hand around my neck, and I lift my head. His lips are there to meet mine, and his hips jut into me. He kisses me with that same devouring hunger that captured me the first time we met.

I want him. He's my husband. Call me a stupid romantic, but that means something to me.

What the fuck can I do to help myself?

The answer sits in my head. It's right there, but it sounds so insane that I'm afraid to look into Jack's puzzled eyes and tell him what I want from him.

If you don't ask him, you'll never know.

I force myself to pull back, and his breath warms my lips. I open my mouth.

"I want a baby."

Jesus Christ.

My face is scorching hot, as though there's a wall of fire in front of me.

"*Excuse me*?"

"I want us to have a kid."

"What the fuck?" he says, between a laugh and a legitimate question.

"I know it sounds crazy—"

"—Yeah," he says, eyes widening. "It does."

I grab his shirt, twisting it in my hands. "I *need* this, Jack."

He backs away from me, his eyebrows somewhere in his hair. "You're serious? You want a kid with me?"

"Yeah, I do."

He turns away from me, deep dimples carving into his mouth. "Why?"

That's a good fucking question.

I take a step forward, hands clenched at my sides. "I know this: I'll never be accepted by the family until I'm pregnant with your kid."

"Jesus Christ!" Jack turns his back on me.

My cheeks burn, this time with rage. I'm furious that he won't take me seriously. I lunge for his arm and force him to turn around. He looks surprised by the desperation on my face.

"It's your cousin, isn't it? You're jealous that she has a baby, and now you want one."

Look, I won't deny that there was a sting of jealousy when I saw how happy they were together, and that sweet baby. I want that, too. This isn't about chasing my dreams—I'm convinced the only way I'll be accepted is if I have children with him.

"Well, yeah, but—no! That's not it!"

He avoids my gaze, shaking his head. "Forget it, Beatrice."

I grab his shoulders and give them a little shake. "What happens to me if something happens to you?"

The question turns in his head and he wrinkles his nose. "What?"

"If you die, what happens to me?"

His eyebrows narrow. "I'm not going to die."

"It could happen."

"*Vaffanculo*! I could trip and break my fucking neck, who gives a shit?"

"*I have nowhere to go.*"

That seems to break through to Jack. He relents, heaving a great sigh. "Johnny would take care of you. He'd give you an allowance."

"You *hate* Johnny. Do you really think he's going to give a damn about my life the moment you're gone?"

Discomfort makes Jack restless. He pushes himself off the wall and glares at me. "He would."

But he sounds so unsure.

"They all hate me. The moment you're gone, they'll hurt me. I know it."

His frosty voice blows over me. "I'm not doing this."

The chilly tone seems to cement the fact that I'm surrounded by people who don't give a damn about me. Maya's unreachable and her husband wants her to have nothing to do with me. If he's gone, I'll be thrown to the wolves.

Club whore.

Their vicious voices reverberate in my head, and my eyes burn as I realize how reluctant Jack was to enter into this arrangement at all. My thoughts race and I reach out for him as I collapse to the floor.

Those guys you overheard will probably be the first to slit your throat.

I'm a club whore. A biker bitch. I'll never be anything more, and if the alliance collapses, I'll be the first to go. Why keep someone alive who can run to the police and tell them that she was coerced into marrying one of their members, in order to avoid testifying against the alibi in court? I'd be disposed of the moment I was no longer needed. The mob wouldn't give a shit about the biker wife made from a sham marriage.

Huge sobs wrack from my chest as I kneel on the floor, the weight of everything crushing me down. I hate crying like this—hate feeling out of control.

"They have no respect for me! They won't care about throwing me away!"

Strong hands grip my arms, lifting me up, but I sink back down. Jack lowers to my level and my tears run over his hands as he cups my cheeks. I can't bear to look at him.

"Of course they do. You're my wife."

My voice lifts to the ceiling, hysterical. "You didn't hear them! They said one dead biker wasn't enough—they called me a cunt!"

Jack's face turns ashen. "What? When was this?"

"When I was at the bar with Maya. I don't t-think they knew I was sitting right there."

He stands up slowly and steps away from me, all fatigue gone from his movements. I'm surprised at the violence with which he rips open the closet door to grab his jacket, shrugging it on.

"Where are you going?"

I flinch at his face, which is taut with rage. He moves stiffly and grabs my arms, giving me a brusque kiss on my cheek.

"Don't worry about it."

JACK

Don't worry about it. It's the mantra of wise guys everywhere. I can't tell you how many times I've told that to a woman. Don't worry about it. Everything's fine.

Even when they're not. Especially when they're not.

I had to leave before I exploded, but I don't even slam the car door when I get out. I save that shit for those three guys—I know exactly who they are. She never left my sight the entire time we were at that dinner. I couldn't help but look for her. She's smoking hot and there are plenty of assholes who would hit on her.

A roar builds in my ears as I open the door to the venue, but my heart is steady like a persistent drumbeat. My eyes dart all over the place, looking for those familiar faces so that I can fucking kill them. Instead I see Sal, seated at the dinner table. The live band strikes up a slow ballad, and everyone dances.

I hurry down the steps and kneel at Sal's side.

"Hey! You're back—"

"Tim, Brad, and Vito—where the fuck are they?"

Sal's portly face stumbles. "Uh—they're near the stage, I think."

I look, scanning through the dance floor of couples, and I see the three bastards heckling the lead singer.

"What're you—?"

I ignore the last part of his sentence and grab an empty wine bottle just sitting on the table. Blackness pricks at the edge of my vision.

They called my wife a cunt.

They won't know what hit them.

I get about two feet from them before one of them notices me, and I swing back with the bottle. Vito's head makes a dull sound as the glass shatters down his face. He drops instantly.

"What the fuck?"

The music shrieks. Brad grabs my arm and I elbow his face hard. Then an arm chokes my neck from behind, and I see Brad's nose streaming with blood. I slip out of the chokehold and Tim screams at me.

"Fucking moron!"

My fist whirls at his face, and he ducks. Then a blow to the back of my head sends me reeling forward.

Turn around!

My balance is off and pain explodes over my skull. Tim's fist swings at me. I grab his arm and yank. He flies right into my raised knee and his huge moan echoes in the venue. Someone grabs my middle and I dive toward the stage, groping until I take something long and metallic. It's heavy. The bronze flashes across my vision as I swing it in my hands, bashing against the side of Brad's face. It makes a loud, gong-like sound. I realize I grabbed the fucking trombone.

"FUCK!"

"That's mine, you dick!"

I look up into the musician's hostile face, exploding. "Why don't you come down here and I'll cram it up your ass?"

Something appears from the corner of my vision. I duck, the bat whistling over my head. I lunge at him before he can swing it again and hit him hard right below his ribs.

He makes a retching sound and then my fist crunches the side of his head. Brad falls flat on his face, his abdomen heaving, but I can't let the fucker go. I know what he said to her. Beatrice's crying face surfaces in my vision and a fresh wave of fury makes me kick the asshole while he's down. That's what they did to her, didn't they?

"Jack! What the FUCK?"

Johnny's stern voice incenses me. A corrosive hatred that I've never known rises inside me. I can't touch him, so I whale on Brad. My boot crunches his face. I get down on the floor and take a fistful of hair, and—someone tackles me.

"Let me the fuck go!"

"Take him out of here," I hear Johnny mutter.

Three men grab hold of my arms and drag away from Brad, escorting me through the wall of people, who scream when I approach.

"Everything's fine. Go back to your tables."

I almost laugh at the sound of forced calm in Johnny's voice.

My arms twist behind my back as they throw me outside some Employees Only exit, which empties into a deserted lot. Johnny explodes from the door, grabbing my collar.

"What the fuck was that?"

"They called my wife a cunt!"

Suck my dick, asshole.

He jabs at my chest. "What the hell are you talking about?"

"They made comments about my wife in her presence. Get the fuck off me!" I yank my arms out of their grips and glare at Johnny, who looks slightly mollified.

"So you decide to beat the shit out of them in front of a hundred fucking civilians?" His screams deafen my ears. "You should have told *me* about it, and I would've handled it."

Bullshit.

"So if someone called your wife a biker cunt, you would what?"

He laughs, his white teeth flashing. "Don't even start with me, Jack."

"What?" I scream. "You want to sweep this under the rug, too?"

Johnny's eyes gleam dangerously as he takes a few steps closer. "I wish Mike were here to tell you to shut your fucking mouth."

"He's not here because of you!"

Suddenly a cold muzzle presses against my forehead and Johnny leans in, pressing the barrel against my head as spittle flies from his mouth.

"You want to fucking die? Say one more fucking word."

My heart pounds as I look down the length of the muzzle, down the arm, wishing I could tell him how much I despise him.

"I'd kill you if I didn't need you."

"John—hold on. Just relax." Sal suddenly edges in beside John, and I feel a rush of gratitude.

"You realize our relationship with the Devils is hanging by a fucking thread?" John clenches his teeth, his fingers white knuckling the gun. "I am *not* going to prison."

Sal gives me a warning look. "His temper got a little out of hand, but I wouldn't say it wasn't justified."

"I don't give a fuck." He slowly lowers the gun, his chest pulsing hard. "Tommy, Rick."

They seize my arms as Johnny slips the gun back into his jacket pocket. I screw up my face as Rick steps behind me, twisting my arms back.

Tommy shrugs apologetically as he raises a fist and slams it into my shoulder.

"FUCK!"

The scream tears from my throat as I feel the massive blow radiating pain down my arm. Another pinpointed hit thuds against my bones. They scrape against each other and I press my lips together, willing myself not to cry out.

"That's for being a complete prick at my dinner."

Even though my shoulder screams in pain, I lift myself up. Unbridled heat sears through my veins. "I would do it again. She's my wife."

Johnny sneers at me. "You're defending a girl you didn't even want to fucking marry."

That's true, but I can't pretend that I didn't feel something for her when she talked about the MC, and when she collapsed into tears at my place. A strange pain twisted inside me, similar to the pain my brother's death gave me.

"*That girl* belongs to me and they insulted me by trashing her. I should kill them."

His cool eyes cut mine. "They'll be dealt with, but I won't let you kill them."

What?

"Are you fucking kidding me?"

He makes a violent movement and slams his fist into my shoulder. Sal holds me back as pain burns through my joint like a white-hot poker, searing.

"Get the fuck out of here!" He screams in my face, apoplectic with rage. "Take your wife and go somewhere else before I do something I regret."

Gladly.

Johnny motions his head, and they release my arms. Fuck, the pain. The slick bastard walks back toward the entrance, leaving me alone with Sal, whose anxious, round face turns to me. He doesn't speak until the door closes, leaving us alone outside.

"John's a cunthair from blowing your head off. What's the matter with you?"

I shake off his hand, trembling slightly with the pain radiating down my arm. Then the rage suddenly burns out. What's all this anger done for me except put my head on the chopping block? And if I go, so does she. Three people dead for no reason.

I can't go on like this.

"I can't do this anymore." Everything keeps feeding into my rage, making me sick to my stomach.

"Jack, we'll find out who was responsible. I swear to God. If it really was John—"

"I'll never find out."

And I sure as shit can't kill a boss.

"Jack!"

I just want to go home. "I'll drive myself home."

My thoughts churn as I walk away from Sal's voice, the uncomfortably warm night clinging to my skin. I reach my car, shoulder burning, and sit in there for a while.

The night sky is clear.

Wouldn't it be nice to just let go?

An image of my brother, straight backed and proud, flashes through my vision. He always wore that slightly sarcastic grin. Impatient, prone to yell, but loyal to a fault.

There was nobody but him for all the Christmases. Him and the family. I remember one of the captains dressing up as Santa Claus when I was younger and handing out gifts to all the kids. I felt like I belonged somewhere, but Mike was tethering me there. Without him, I was lost.

I stop my car in front of my apartment, almost at peace. I can almost fucking see the stars, and then Johnny's cold face flashes in front of my vision. He bends over Mike's hospital bed with the pillow, after bribing the nurses to look away, and holds it over Mike's mouth.

My fingers tighten over the steering wheel so hard that I can hear the leather squeak. I can't let it go.

I open the door and slide out, slamming the door shut before taking the steps two at a time. Beatrice suddenly flames in my vision.

Looking at me with wide blue eyes. Begging me to knock her up.

I jam my keys inside the lock and burst into my apartment. My heart pounds when I see her seated at the kitchen table, waiting for me.

I know what I fucking want, and it's her.

She gets up from the table, wearing another one of my shirts and nothing else, probably because she wants to lure me into fucking her without a condom because all of a sudden, she wants my baby.

And there's something incredibly hot about that.

"Jack, what happened? Your shoulder!"

Fuck my shoulder.

I stride into the kitchen, blood pounding so hard I can barely hear a thing. My hand wraps in her hair and I take her mouth. Her soft lips yield under mine and she slides her arms around my neck. The bottom of the t-shirt lifts, exposing a line of her creamy stomach. My dick hardens, throbbing with an intense urge for something warm and wet. It's just there, hidden under those thin cotton panties she's not supposed to wear.

My fingers dig into her hair as she leans into me, her tits brushing against my chest, and then I pull back.

"I'll give you what you want."

"Really?"

"Yeah."

Her eyes bead with happy tears and she touches my face, her thumbs trailing the edge of my smile.

"But you can't leave me."

"I won't."

"No matter what happens between the MC and the mob, you're mine."

"Thank you."

My cock jumps in my pants when her soft lips crush mine. Her eagerness makes my dick throb, but I pull back.

"Thank me after I've filled you with my cum."

Then I bend down and pick her up in my arms. My arm feels like it's ripping in half, but I carry her to the bedroom and let her down on the mattress gently.

Beatrice looks up at me with a shy smile, her golden hair splayed over the black t-shirt she wears.

I've never done this before and my dick is hard enough to pound nails. There's something exciting about it. She's desperate for my cum, and God knows I love giving it to her.

I drop my slacks and briefs, cold air hitting my dick as I tear my shirt from my body. Her shirt flies from her head, revealing her perfect tits. A switch inside my brain flips and suddenly I'm on the bed, grabbing a fistful of her panties and tearing them from her legs.

A stream of pre-cum slides down my cock, and before I can let myself go, I look into her anxious eyes.

"I'm going to claim your body the way I should've on our wedding night."

"Do it. Fuck me."

She breathes it out as though it's a thrill. I see it in her eyes and in the burn on her cheeks.

I launch forward. I can't fucking take it anymore. Need to be buried balls deep into that pussy that glistens for me. I watch the shock on her face as I spread her apart with my cock, feeling her warmth hugging me tightly for the first time. Feeling her completely raw like this takes my breath away, and for a moment I stay sheathed inside her. Her legs wrap around me, and I pull back and thrust hard again, feeling her breath hitch. She reaches down my back, making my skin burn, and digs her nails into my bare ass.

"Beg for my cum."

I lean back, pausing my thrusts to fondle her swollen tits. I bend over, sucking her into my mouth as she arches her back, crying.

"More. I want more, please."

I flatten myself over her, my elbows on each side of her head as she bites her lip and digs her nails into me. It feels different. Somehow that thin piece of latex separated something a lot bigger than just a patch of skin. She's not just some girl I married to save my ass anymore. She's my wife. She's going to carry my kid.

I wrap my arm around her back and the ache running along my cock grows, ever persistent. I ram my hips into her, loving the sound of her wet pussy smacking against my balls. A moan rips from her throat and excitement shoots up my chest.

"I'll fuck our baby into you, but you have to come first."

Beatrice's feverish eyes find mine. "Keep going. Don't stop."

I don't think I could ever stop.

The pressure builds up behind the ache, and Beatrice edges it along with every yell she makes to urge me faster. *Fuck me. Come inside me.*

Then finally she tightens her arms around my neck and falls apart, the tension loosening from her face as she comes.

I crush my body against hers and wrench her head toward me, tasting her minty breath as I moan in between kissing her. My hips dig in deep. I fuck her so goddamn hard the headboard smashes against the wall. Then I feel it rippling from me and I thrust so hard that she gasps. I yell into her lips but she keeps kissing me, and I feel my cock soaking her womb with my cum. An inexplicably mind-blowing feeling washes over me. My hips move of their own accord, pulsing into her as streams of cum continue to jet. I've never fucked a woman bareback before.

It's fucking awesome.

I keep myself deep inside her, breathing hard as Beatrice runs her hands through my hair. She smiles at me. It's such a beautiful thing that I forget myself for a moment. Then she pulls me down closer and breathes thanks into my lips.

A light, dizzy feeling fills my head as she kisses me hard, my muscles spasming. She massages the base of my neck and my chest tightens, heart hammering. God, I can't get enough of her. I slide a hand underneath her head and kiss her hard as my dick swells inside her. Why do I want this so badly? I search my feelings, but I can't begin to clear the fog clouding my brain. I just know that I want to keep coming inside her and no one else. As many times as it takes until that stick changes color or whatever the fuck it is.

She runs her fingers along my jaw and keeps staring at me as though I'm her goddamn savior. I find I don't mind it so much.

"You happy?"

"Yes."

Her grin is so wide you'd think I gave her ten orgasms.

"I want this. I've wanted kids since I was a girl."

I can't say I felt the same. Even now it's hard to imagine, but what better way to give a middle fucking finger to the MC than to knock up one of their women?

"Good, because your pussy is going to milk my cock every day." I dig my hips into her and she gasps.

Her freckles burn a deep red and I bend my head, kissing her cheeks.

You're not just a biker bitch.

We're way past that shit. I'm balls deep inside her, fully intending to knock her up and make her mine. She touches my face, the blue in her eyes seeming to spill from her irises. Then her pale eyelashes blink and the tears cling to tiny strands.

She gives me that look I recognize from some women—that starved, hopeless look that tugs at me. A finger touches my swollen shoulder.

"What happened to you?"

I shrug, and the movement sends pain stabbing through my muscles. "Forget about it."

"You went back to the club, didn't you?"

"Yeah, and I beat the shit out of some assholes."

She makes a heavy sound but doesn't frown. "I didn't ask you to do that."

"Since when do I do what you say?" I give her hip a rough pinch. "You're my wife. They called you a cunt. Most guys get killed for that."

"I don't want anyone to die."

I trail a finger up and down her neck. "How do you grow up in the MC and not accept that things like this happen all the time?"

The blaze disappears from her eyes and she sinks back into the sheets, looking so down that I feel like an asshole for rubbing it in her face.

"I'm going to have a lot of fun with you the next couple weeks."

"Couple weeks?"

"Yeah, I've got some time off. Plenty of time to get you knocked up. Anywhere you want to go?"

Her eyes widen. "What do you mean?"

"It'd be nice to get the fuck out of here for a while."

"I've never been out of Montreal." An electric smile lights up her face. "What about Vegas?"

"What's in Vegas?" I say with a laugh.

"Shows, gambling—"

"—Hookers, strip clubs. I like where you're going with this."

She gives me a soft punch. "Stop being an ass."

"Relax. We'll go." I lay a kiss on her shocked face. "I'll have to tell friends of ours that I'm in the area, but we'll go."

"Jack, we could not come back—if you wanted."

Take off to another country, never look back? Never find out who destroyed my life?

"I can't just leave."

Leaving this place would feel like leaving my brother behind, and everything that happened. I can't do that.

She doesn't say a thing, just watches me with that anxious look that I hate.

I'm not giving up, Mike.

* * *

Vegas is an epileptic nightmare. Giant billboards flash with eyeball-searing brightness, blotting out the night. Assholes in stupid character costumes dance in the sidewalks, trying to get pictures for cash. Stripper cards scatter over the sidewalks like confetti. I step over hundreds of cards with naked girls flashing their tits to the camera, and I realize that the last time I've fucked another girl was weeks ago. Weeks.

I went from a douchebag sleeping my way across the city to trying to knock up my wife.

What happened?

Some jerk snaps his stack of cards at me, and I wave him off. Jesus Christ—do I look like a guy who pays for pussy?

It's unbelievably hot, even at this time of night. The heat makes my eyes feel warm. It evaporates the sweat almost immediately, and I'm wearing slacks and a dress shirt because she wanted to dress up.

"Oh my God, that's amazing!"

Beatrice grasps my arm and forces me to stop, pointing out something that I've seen dozens of times before—a Michael Jackson impersonator.

Okay, fine. He looks pretty good.

My heart thuds when she curls an arm around my waist and kisses my cheek.

"Thank you for bringing me here."

She squeezes me again and moves from my side, getting lost in all the glamour. I walk behind her, hands deep in my pockets, right underneath the flashing pink and yellow Flamingos Casino. I watch her shake her cute ass in that dark-purple dress I bought her. Apparently it was a designer brand. I just liked the way her tits looked in the dress. Beatrice's blonde hair flies as she turns around, giving me a sweet smile. It tugs at my chest and I smile back.

Fine. I'll admit that I like her. It's comforting to have her with me. Even more comforting inside her, after I've fucked myself into exhaustion.

I don't drink as much anymore.

Fuck.

Weeks ago I couldn't get through a night without something, and ever since she came into my life, I haven't really.

You replaced one vice with another.

Two guys wearing polos take long looks at my wife after walking past her. She doesn't notice a goddamn thing. My perfect, innocent little wife.

I grab her waist and force her to stop, and then I bury my hand in her hair and I make her kiss me, right in the middle of the sidewalk. People walk around us, but I just feel her. Taste her. Her cheeks are rosy when I finally break away from her soft lips. Jesus Christ, she's hot. I have a hard time tearing my eyes from the deep V-neck and those creamy tits on display for me.

"I'm going to fuck you in that little dress."

I take her hand and drag her across the street, the heat baking my back as we make our way into our gilded hotel. She looks longingly at the crowd of slot machines in the lobby blinking blue lights. Entranced, she stares at it until I tug her into the elevator. The gleaming doors slide open, mirroring Beatrice's happy face, and then I open the door to our suite.

It's fucking huge.

She presses her palms to the dark windows overlooking the strip. Her hair flashes as she turns around, beaming.

"This is incredible!"

I smile at her and roll our suitcases into the bedroom, and then I walk in the bathroom. Light beams over polished white marble. I take a leak and when I get out, I almost slip on something.

It's the dress she was wearing.

Smiling to myself, I pick it up and glance down the hall, spotting another piece of crumpled fabric on the floor.

My wife is desperate for cock.

I walk to it, picking up her bra. It still smells like her. God, I can just picture her waiting somewhere for me.

A black thong sits on the kitchen counter. I take it, feeling her warmth lingering on the fabric. Shit, where is she? How many goddamn rooms does this place have?

I follow the articles of clothing, which lead to a glass door to the outdoors. The warm air hits me immediately as I slide it open. The terrace is huge, and there's a flickering orange light. It makes the shadows tremble.

I round some hedges and see a fire pit, the orange flames licking over fake logs. Surrounding the fire pit is outdoor furniture, including a red couch. A naked woman lies on the couch, her tits like round globes on her chest. Her cascade of blonde hair shifts across her face as she moves her head.

Blood pounds so thickly in my veins that I can't hear anything but a roar. My cock stands to attention as I walk closer to that perfect vision of her, bare underneath the sky. It's fucking hot out, especially with that fire, but I can't see her without its light.

I tug at my shirt collar, unbuttoning it slowly as she stares up at me. Then I can't take looking at her anymore. I have to run my hands all over my woman.

"All this to get me to fuck you?" I spread my hand over her smooth belly.

Jesus, just look at her legs. She folds them neatly to the side so that I can't see her pussy, just a tantalizing V. Beatrice smiles with a shy, "Who, me?" expression.

She knows exactly what she's doing.

I kneel down and curve my hand around her tits, squeezing. She lets out a small noise, and then I suck her hard nipple. I flick my tongue across it as she inhales a sharp gasp, and then my teeth graze her.

"You want a baby so fucking bad, don't you?"

"Yeah."

"You want a baby like other people want puppies. Your body just wants to fuck, sweetheart. I'm all right with that."

"Don't mock me."

I ignore her, continuing on. "You want a screaming little bastard to wake you up every couple hours for months on end?"

She sits up. "*Yes.*"

I agreed to get her pregnant out of lust. My dick loves the idea, but my brain? The part of me that still loves freedom? I keep thinking of her getting big with my seed inside her, and my cock won't shut the fuck up.

Fuck her. Fuck her. Fuck her.

"What the hell am I getting out of this?"

"You get a *child.*"

A child. I picture it in my head—a small blonde boy careening into my knees and wrapping chubby arms around my legs, saying "Daddy!"

There's a twinge in my chest.

"I want a baby with *you*, no one else."

The flames flicker in her eyes. She leans forward and touches my cock. It's embarrassing how quickly it grows in her hands. Goddamn her.

"I know you just want my cum and you'll do anything to get it."

And I'm willing to let you.

She ignores me and sits up, undoing my button and unzipping my slacks as she cups my balls. My slacks fall down my legs and she leans forward, kissing my thickening cock. It makes it twitch and blood rushes to my head.

"Is that such a bad thing?"

Frankly I don't give a shit if she's nuts for a baby. She's literally begging me to fuck her. I can't say no.

Beatrice drags my briefs down over my ass, until my dick springs free. She fists it and I sigh at the contact as I feel the heat from the fire on the backs of my legs. Her pink mouth inches forward, and I move my hips so that my cock slides against her lips. The warmth of her mouth swallows me and I watch as she sits neatly on her legs. Her tits bounce slightly as she jerks her arm and slides her tongue all over me. I grab the back of her head, already feeling the ache build up like fire. Irritating. Burning.

She sucks my cock like a popsicle, slurping noisily. She moans as though she really enjoys it, and she does. I can see the bright sheen of juice on her pussy.

I dig my hands into her hair and sigh when my cock slides all the way inside her throat. Her nose brushes my skin.

"Careful, or you're going to get it in your mouth instead."

My cock throbs with the need to bury it somewhere where it'll do some good. Right in that pussy begging for me. I pop out of her mouth and the cool air hits my wet dick. She stands up and grabs my tie, and I'm just barely holding myself back from grabbing her fucking hair and throwing her over the couch.

She pulls my tie and her lips brush against my ear. "I want you.

Not just for this." She grabs my cock and gives it a squeeze. "Because you're strong. You don't take shit from anybody."

Jesus Christ, I can't think when she's stroking my cock, and then suddenly warmth blazes under my skin. I still see the biker girl I was forced to marry. There's still poison in my gut.

And I want to fuck her until she's no longer recognizable. I want my kid growing inside her. Make me marry your biker bitch? Fine, but I'm not giving her back.

I take a fistful of her hair and lead her over the arm over the couch. I push her porcelain body until her ass is positioned perfectly, and then I rip a hand across her cheek. She spreads her legs apart and I slide my thick cock along her pussy, feeling her shiver.

It makes my blood rush to my groin. It's so easy to just slip my cock into her pussy and feel the head slowly part her open for me, but I don't.

"Don't be a jackass. Just fuck me!"

I swallow my laughter. "You're right that I don't take shit from anybody. That includes you, sweetheart."

I lean over and press my lips to her swollen cheek, and then I bite down hard. She squeals in pain, and I pull back, seeing the bite mark on her ass. Perfect.

"I'm sorry!"

"Good girl."

And the side of her face that I can see collapses with relief. It makes me laugh. What a submissive little girl.

Then I slide my cock back to her clenching pussy. I push slowly.

Her body shudders with a sigh as I enter her with just one inch. She tries to buck against me, but I flatten my palm against her back.

"Please—don't tease me."

"You'll take my cock and shut up, or you'll get nothing."

I grin at her back. Basically it's an empty threat, but she clams up anyway. I shove another inch inside and then I withdraw completely. It's fucking painful for me. She bites her lip viciously.

"I changed my mind. I want to hear you beg."

"Please, Jack!" she gasps. "I don't know why you do this. I do everything you tell me to do."

Everything and more.

"I love seeing you like this. You have no idea how hot it is to have some slut on all fours, begging for your cum."

She stands up and turns around in my arms. I grab her wrists. She's flushed with redness, even the skin above her tits.

"I want you, goddamn it! Stop teasing and fuck me!"

She hits my chest, and it's not hard enough to hurt me. Her voice echoes in the terrace. I respond by curling my hand in her hair and yanking her back into place. I throw her over the arm again and fist my cock, aiming it right at her pussy. Then I shove hard. She lets out a yell. She squeezes around me and I pull back and hammer her again, giving her no time to adjust.

"This is what you want?"

"Yes, please! Harder!"

I'll fuck you harder, bitch.

I grab her hips and thrust with all my strength. She bounces against me and I yank back, that amazing thrill shooting into my dick more, the deeper I bury myself. I love seeing her ass bounce on my cock, and the way her tits sway back and forth with the violence of my thrusts. Her throat tears into the night so that I think all of Vegas can probably hear us fucking.

I reach for her hair spilling all over her back and I grab those silky strands, pulling her hard enough to make her legs shake.

Then I look down and see my cock, slick with her pussy juice, pummeling her. I hold her hips and jar her body, keeping myself balls deep. It rips from me. Cum blasts from my dick and she grinds her hips against me, taking it all.

Fuck. Holy fuck it feels so good.

I pulse a few more times, feeling my dick shooting inside her. My legs shake as exhaustion settles in. I pull out, and she puts her hand inside her pussy. That greedy girl wants to keep all of my cum inside her.

I lie down, settling in behind her as I curl my hand around her stomach. I nuzzle her neck and give her a kiss as pleasure numbs every thought.

Beatrice turns her head and I catch her parted lips, slipping my tongue inside her sweet mouth. She sighs into me and I pull back from her, every surface of my body tingling.

Then she pulls back, looking at me. "Why did you say yes?"

"I can't bring my brother back, but maybe I can make a family with you."

Her eyes slowly well up and a horrible feeling clenches my

stomach.

"What did I say?"

"I'm sorry about your brother," she chokes out. "I hate what they did to you. I hate the violence between our families. I want it to stop."

Tears slip down her face as she silently cries.

I don't have the heart to tell her that it won't ever stop.

BEATRICE

Heat lines ripple over the concrete like waves of water. The strip of sunlight across my shoulder slowly burns my skin, and I shift myself so that I'm covered by the umbrella. Even in the extreme heat, Jack looks cool. He wears a white button-up shirt, the sleeves rolled up, and slacks. His hair looks static in the nonexistent breeze. A tray of breakfast separates us. Jack reaches across the table and holds out his hand. I slip mine into his and he gives me a wink that makes me feel giddy, as though I've had a big sip of wine. Every time he looks at me and smiles, I can't help but feel like a girl with a stupid crush.

A soft jangling sound shatters the peaceful morning, and Jack slips his hand into his slacks to retrieve his cell phone. He frowns at the screen.

"Yeah? Hey, Sal." He pauses for a moment. "Yeah, it's nice. One second." He moves the phone from his face and addresses me. "I have to take this."

My mood sours as Jack rises from the table and walks away from the table and down the edge of the pool.

I think about that night we talked about the violence in our families. If I get pregnant, I'll become one of them. But Jack's brother died at the hands of the mob. His own people. Are we really safe?

The sun disappears and a cloud rolls over my body, chilling me instantly. Suddenly I long for home. Those four concrete walls were confining, but I never felt scared behind them.

A hand curls over my shoulder and I jump in my seat.

"Relax." Jack pulls up his chair and sits beside me. "There's some things I have to take care of."

"*What*? Why?"

He lifts up his shoulder in a shrug, looking irritated. "John just wants me to check in with some people here."

I grab his arm. "Doesn't he know you're still injured?"

His eyes narrow. "I'm sure he doesn't give a shit." His tone softens when he sees the anxiety on my face. "It's not going to be like that. Don't worry."

"Can't you see that he keeps sending you places that get you hurt?" My voice drops and I feel my cheeks flush.

He laughs. "Sweetheart, if he wanted to kill me he'd just fucking do it."

I dig my nails into his arm. "Not if he knew the rest of the guys wouldn't approve. Like your brother."

Jack's face darkens and he pulls his arm out from under mine. "Beatrice, you need to relax. I'll be back in a few hours."

He stands up and kisses my head, giving me a small smile before he walks away.

Sighing, I sit back into my chair and pick a few more strawberries from the pile on my plate, watching the rippling blue waves of the pool. I decide to walk down the strip on my own to kill time before Jack gets back.

The sun beats down on my neck as I walk across the huge

traverses, passing by Caesar's Palace. I wander in some of the shops, and I stop in my tracks when I see a tattoo parlor.

An idea makes my heart flutter.

Yes.

It's fucking crazy.

He'll love it.

I open the glass door to the tattoo parlor, and a redheaded girl with colorful koi fish tattoos spiraling her arms looks up at me with a smile.

"Hi, I'd like a tattoo."

"Great! What were you looking to do?"

"Something small. Just text. Do you have any availability?"

"Yeah, come in."

I walk behind the counter, my heart beating faster as I prepare myself to tell her what I want. Just a line of text, really.

She grins wickedly. "I'm assuming Jack is your husband?"

"Yes."

"Are you sure you want to do this?"

"*Yes.*"

It's not that crazy. Women in the MC do it all the time for their husbands, but it sure as hell isn't a requirement. My insides boil with excitement. It's reckless and completely unlike me, but I know I'll never be with anyone else.

Maybe this is my way of telling him that.

I lie on the bench after rolling down my panties and jeans. The needle slices into the skin in my back, right above where he loves to spank me. I grit my teeth against the pain.

Suck it up. Girls in the MC do this all the damn time.

It only takes about an hour, and then she makes me stand up and gives me a mirror. The elegant script wraps around my hip, dancing right over my cheek.

"He's going to love it. Thank you so much."

"No problem!"

She wraps it up and I walk to the front to pay, my skin smarting a little.

"Have a good time tonight!" she calls after me when I leave the store.

"Thanks, I will!"

I dig my phone from my purse and see a few text messages. We're going out gambling as soon as we get back, and he wants me to dress up.

A slow smile spreads across my face.

* * *

The tattoo fucking *burns.*

The pain smarts as I lie on the couch, and I fight the urge to get up and look at the sprawling black ink in the bathroom mirror again. Fuck, it looks awesome.

It's a pretty fucking crazy move to tattoo anyone's name to your body, isn't it?

That's mainstream opinion, but I grew up in the MC, expecting to become someone's old lady one day. I watched dozens of women get branded with their husband's name and waited for the day where the same would happen to me.

Jack might not understand it, but this is my way of fusing our cultures together.

A jolt of excitement runs through my body as I hear him fiddling with the door, and I sit bolt upright, tugging my skirt over my knees.

"Beatrice?" he says, his voice echoing in the huge suite. "Are you ready?"

I stand up as his footsteps echo in the living room, his powerful voice sending a shiver down my spine. Then I see him, silhouetted in the doorway.

"I'm here."

He turns his head and sees me standing there. "Well, come on. We have a VIP game to get to."

I walk closer to him, studying the way his suit wraps around his body like silk. The dark-blue fabric makes his skin shine, and I think about those powerful muscles—his thick thighs hiding underneath.

Damn, he looks hot in a suit.

My hands reach out, touching his chest. I slide between his jacket and feel the broad muscles, and then I move up to play with his neck. Jack shuts his eyes, sucking in breath. He looks so made up and handsome that I have to taste him. The closer I am, the more powerless I feel, until my mouth falls on his. He kisses me before biting me softly.

"Baby—"

"I just want to show you something first."

An uncertain smile staggers across his face. "Okay."

Then I pull the hem of the skirt down until I feel it drag over the raw flesh.

"What the hell are you doing?"

"I got a tattoo."

He lifts the back of my shirt and lets out a choked laugh. "Holy fuck. What does it say—*Property of Jack*?"

He rips my skirt down and his hand curves around my ass. "So your ass belongs to me?"

I can't help but smile at that. "Yeah, along with the rest of me."

He squeezes me. "Jesus."

"You like it, then?"

Possessive hands dig into my hips and he gives my ass a sharp slap. "You knew damn well I would."

I feel the evidence pressing against my leg.

"I keep picturing nailing you from behind while this is staring me in the face. Fuck, Beatrice."

I love the grittiness in his voice when he hauls me upright, his hand still on my ass. The way his eyes gleam sends a thrill into my core, and then he kisses me. His tongue shoves down my throat, and I cling to him. A frustrated growl rocks through my clit.

"I can't fuck you right now, so I'll fuck you during the game."

Wait, *what*?

"I *told* you not to tease me."

"Jack, how are you going to—ah!"

He rips my underwear with one quick jerk. He actually tears them from my thighs and stuffs them in his jacket pocket.

"I'm going to fuck you in front of all those men, and they won't even know it."

What?

I try not to laugh at the maniacal grin on Jack's face and I pull my skirt back up.

"Let's go."

He slides an arm around my waist, muttering something under his breath with a throaty growl.

"You little bitch," he says in a husky voice, bending down to nip my ear. "I'm going to make you pay."

Whatever.

I've no idea what the hell he's talking about. Jack's sexual tastes are pretty wild, but I doubt he'd actually fuck me in front of a room filled with people.

We leave the suite and take the elevator down. As soon as the doors close, his mouth is on the top of my breasts, sucking hard.

"Jack!"

My back hits the wall as he pins me there, sucking so hard that he leaves a bright, wet mark behind. He appreciates it for a moment and swipes his thumb across it. The feeling of his tongue on my tits lingers there, pounding between my legs as he watches me with a dark smile.

"That's just the beginning."

The elevator doors open and I catch a glimpse of myself, flustered and red, that mark burning on my chest.

Damn it.

I follow him outside, lust raging through my limbs as he takes me through the maze of the casino.

"It's a high-stakes game. Texas Hold'em." Jack turns, a wicked grin on his face. "Shouldn't be more than a couple hours."

What the hell is he talking about?

I'm distracted by the noise in the casino. God, it's loud. The constant roar blasts my ears and everywhere there's something to look at—a bright screen, numbers flashing.

My heart gallops as he takes me through a set of doors leading to a small, stuffy room with a single poker table. Five men already seated at the table look up and smile at Jack, who steps away from me slightly.

"This is my wife, Beatrice. I'm Jack."

I lean over the large table, shaking hands with an old man whose papery skin pulls into a smile.

They introduce themselves and I forget their names almost instantly.

Did he say he was going to fuck me during the game? Not possible. No way.

But a tinge of lingering doubt makes the smile on my face strained.

He sits down and looks up at me, patting his lap.

Seriously?

"C'mon. Don't be shy."

He grabs my wrist and drags me, slipping his arms around my waist. He yanks me backward and I fall over his legs, my face burning as he tugs me against his chest. My pulse thunders in my ears as he adjusts himself. Then his lips singe the flesh on my neck. He kisses me, gentle and sweet. Or it would be if it weren't for his hand curving around my upper thigh.

Is he fucking serious?

We're seated at the poker table in close quarters with everyone else. Henry, the investment banker who sits next to us, focuses his gaze on the cards flipping in the dealer's hand.

Slowly I slide my hand over his and then I dig my nails into his flesh. In response he moves his hand up my skirt and pinches the sensitive flesh around my upper thigh.

I turn my head ever so slightly and hiss through my teeth. "What the hell are you doing?"

"If you don't sit still and take it like a good girl, you'll take it like a bad girl upstairs."

Then he plants another hot kiss on my cheek, and the hand clutches my thigh greedily. It feels good. Too fucking good. He knows exactly how to get a response from me, and his hand keeps inching up my thigh.

Take it like a bad girl upstairs.

What would that be like? I think back to the first time he bent me over his knee. I remember the swift burn and the way I trembled, anticipating the blow. Then pleasure when he smoothed his hand over my skin.

It almost makes me want to defy him, just so that I can experience that raw, passionate energy. Sometimes it feels good to be taken roughly and fucked hard, and the tattoo I got for him seems to have put Jack in a mood. He can't stop fondling me under the table, and if we weren't at a table full of other men I'd like to relax in his arms and let him have his way with me.

"Gentlemen, it's ten thousand to sit down."

Jesus.

Jack's hand pauses momentarily as he leans forward and grabs a couple chips from the pile in front of him. I notice that they're thousand-dollar chips and hold my breath as the dealer reveals the first couple cards. A nine and a two. Jack's cards are shit. He folds.

I freeze as his finger moves over my skin, and then someone coughs loudly and I jump a little. I feel him exchange something from his other hand, and then a small and hard piece of plastic presses up against my clit.

What the fuck?

His thumb massages the round plastic thing in a circle over my clit as his other fingers slide down, trailing a blaze of fire.

Is he trying to get me off with a fucking chip?

My legs seize as his middle finger slips down a deliciously wet, sensitive area of my pussy. I turn my head to glare at him, but his face is impassive, totally focused on the game.

He slides up and down my pussy as his thumb presses down hard, ramping up the pleasure—the need for something thick to fill me up. My nipples harden into points. He keeps teasing me with the finger, dipping it in and sliding against my clit. Heat builds up right underneath his fingers and my chest feel uncomfortably warm. I wonder what I must look like now. I catch the man across the table looking at me, and I freeze.

"And here's the river."

The dealer flips the last card and two men show their hands. The orthopedic surgeon smiles as he reaches forward, gathering the chips. The loser sinks back into his chair with a small curse.

I squeeze my legs together as his finger slides between my slick walls. An electrical current suddenly hits my clit, singeing up my spine to burrow in my heart. I open my mouth and utter a small gasp.

Shit.

Their heads turn toward me as Jack moves slightly and gives me another kiss in a show of affection that doesn't quite match the embarrassment of being fingered under a fucking table in front of everyone. Luckily they take my gasp for excitement over the game. The man next to us turns his head as Jack slowly pumps his finger in and out. I feel every edge of him entering me. Heat rises up my neck and I clench my thighs together, but I remember his warning.

Take it like a good girl.

I relax my legs.

"So are you guys on vacation?" the man next to us asks conversationally.

His finger anchors hard inside me and I feel my juices slipping around him. Jesus Christ, how am I supposed to keep myself together?

"Actually, we're on our honeymoon."

His voice rumbles through my back as he keeps fucking me,

rubbing hard with that thousand-dollar chip. I can barely think of anything but how good it fucking feels. Jesus Christ, I can't believe he's getting me this hot with a goddamn poker chip. I want more—I want him. Finally I hold his arm, stilling his movements under the table.

"Oh, congratulations!"

"Thanks." I manage a weak smile.

"Not a lot of guys bring their wives to these big games." The dealer looks up from the cards at me.

"I put everything on my business card," the orthopedic surgeon chimes in.

They look at us curiously, but I don't really fucking care at this point. His thumb vigorously rubs the chip over my nub, and I'm trying to keep my mouth shut. I'm also trying not to turn around and grab his fucking tie to scream at him to stop fingering me.

But I don't want him to stop. I want it faster.

"Sounds like your wives carry your balls in their purses."

The table erupts with laughter, and I seize up as another finger sinks into my wet pussy. Holy fuck. I just *can't.* Every sensation hits me hard. Even Jack's soft laughter blowing over my neck. I think of sex. I think of him sinking his teeth into me as he ruts me deep. His tongue making hot circles around my nipple. Sucking. Biting.

"Ass."

"At least my wife knows who's boss. Right, sweetheart?"

He takes my chin in his hands and my cheeks flame as his fingers pump inside me, his eyes full of laughter.

Son of a bitch.

I have a mind to grab his cock in front of all the men, but instead I take his tie and yank his head to me. The guys hoot and cheer as I seal my lips against his. Electricity sparks over my skin as he kisses me back and then I slide my tongue inside his mouth.

I don't care how tacky this looks. Payback.

He pulls back, his face a little red as he bares his teeth in a grimace and ruthlessly shoves his fingers inside me.

"Jesus. Take that to the hotel room!"

The room erupts with a smattering of nervous laughter, and some of the guys stare at Jack with open jealousy.

Jack plays a few more games and I get more and more flustered. Fuck, I'm sitting on his goddamn lap and I can feel his dick riding against my ass. He curves his fingers inside me as I grip his arm and slide my fingers over his rocking hand. I trace his knuckles and feel myself clench over him. His thumb moves aggressively, and I bite my lip hard. I'm going to fucking come. I'm going to—

My body shifts as he leans forward and slides all of his chips toward the center. My body shudders as another finger joins, spreading me open.

"I'm all in."

The men at the table miss the hint of laughter in his voice, but the irony doesn't escape me, not when I'm seconds away from coming. A shudder runs up my leg.

No, not now—please!

I can't even hiss an insult because the room is too quiet. Cards fly from the dealer's hand and Jack takes a sip of his whiskey. Then he twists his hand, pinching my clit with the poker chip as he curves upward. My breath hitches and I bite down my lip. I clench over his fingers and he continues to thrust mercilessly, and I can't help myself. I can't fight the tide of pleasure. A moan shudders from my lips.

It breaks the tension in the room like the crack of a bowling ball on wood. They look at me with raised eyebrows and mild shock, until Jack withdraws his hand from my skirt, wiping himself on my thighs.

"It's a lot of money," I manage to choke out.

Jack seizes the excuse, chuckling slightly. "I told you not to worry about it."

The waves of pleasure cascade over me, weakening my muscles so that I can barely hold myself upright. He slides an arm around my waist and the men return to their game as I try to breathe slow, deep breaths.

"Ah, shit."

I don't even notice that the dealer flipped the last card and that the game is over. The orthopedic surgeon leans across the table and laughs as he rakes in the chips, and Jack makes an elegant shrug. His legs move and we stand up from the table.

"I guess that's it."

I gape at the pile of chips he lost. There's probably thirty grand in there, but it rolls off his shoulders like it's nothing. I feel his heat simmering behind me like a wall of fire, and his hand clenches over my upper arm.

"Nice game."

"Yeah, thanks."

Jack pushes against my side and nearly yanks me from the room. We're thrust into the chaos of the casino as my heart jackknifes in my chest. He pulls me close and I hit the center of his chest as he gives me a smoldering look.

"There's more where that came from, babe."

"Jack, you're *insane.*"

His face lights up with wild laughter as he runs his hands down my body, right over the swell of my ass. "I need to claim my property—now."

My core tightens. "Let's go back."

"I said I wanted you *now.*"

What?

"Jack, we're in a casino."

"The first time we fucked, it was in a VIP room." He presses his lips against my ear, and my body heats up instantly.

"Yeah, but there are cameras all over the place."

He searches the floor, his hunger almost manic. Then he points to a darkened balcony overlooking the casino. It's a restaurant with a big sign indicating that it's under renovations.

"I'm going to fuck you right on that balcony."

The moment he says the word, *fuck*, a tingling sensation spreads over my skin and I know I won't be able to deny him. I've never been able to.

He drags me up the stairs, past the curtained-off rope, and into the darkened, open area. The seats are shoved to the walls and a brass railing gleams over the casino. We're not that high up. A loud noise could attract their attention and they'd just have to look up.

My back hits his chest as he spreads his palm over my stomach and yanks me. "Now I want you to grab ahold of that railing. Don't let go no matter what."

Trembling with excitement, I bend over and grasp the railing as his hands move up my thighs. Cool air hits my skin as he folds the skirt over my back. He grabs the raw flesh where I got inked and thumbs his name.

"Property of Jack… You're damn right you are."

I choke out a yell as a stinging blow lands on my ass. He fingers gouge my flesh, taking a handful of me as he lets out a throaty growl.

"You knew when I saw the tattoo I'd go fucking crazy."

With his other hand he rips my shirt down, the straps falling from my arms as he exposes my tits to the entire casino. He pulls the fabric so that it rests underneath and makes them bulge.

Then he slaps my inner thigh and I spread my legs, wondering how the fuck he convinced me to do this. It's really only fifteen or twenty feet from the group. Close enough to see the gleam of the dealer's earrings.

"Jack, they're going to hear us!"

"Then you better keep quiet."

SLAP!

Another swift blow lands on my ass, stinging the raw tattoo. I bite my lip as the burn spreads to my other cheek. My arms tremble as he spanks me, the sound cracking through the air. It's so loud that I think I see a few of the guests turning around for the source of the sound, and then his hand rips across my tattoo and a painful moan shakes from my mouth.

His hardness digs into my ass as he leans into me, wrapping his arms around my legs greedily. A line of pleasure runs down my spine to the hot glow in my pussy.

"You feel how goddamn hard I am?"

"Yeah."

I want to feel that thickness—want to wrap my fingers around him and own that part of him, but I know my orders.

Don't let go no matter what.

My nipples harden into studs as his body slides up behind me. He moves his leg between mine and his muscles flex, pushing them farther apart. Blood churns under the very surface of my skin. I'm completely exposed, tits hanging out of my shirt for everyone to see.

His pants drop and then I feel the heat of his cock flat against my ass. "I don't think I've ever been this turned-on in my life. Seeing my name right there—Jesus Christ, I *can't*—"

His growl reverberates through my body as he grabs a handful of me and squeezes.

"Jack, please. Let's get this over with."

"Get this over with?" he explodes. "Excuse me?"

Oh shit.

"You think I'm just here to get my dick wet, don't you?"

"No—"

"I'm more than just a load in your cunt. I'm your fucking

husband."

The brand with his name explodes with pain again, and I cry out. I swear to God, I see some of the heads lifts below us.

"I—I know that. Please—"

"Then shut up and don't rush me. I'll take my sweet time claiming you. It's my right."

I start to protest, and then he slips his thick cock in between my aching lips. It slides forward and his throbbing head pokes out between my legs. Jesus Christ. Below us a throng of people scream with excitement at the craps table and the noise sends a thrill through me.

He reaches around my hips and grabs himself, making sure he rides my pussy hard. Hot air blows over my neck, and then his teeth sink into my flesh briefly. "Just for that I'm going to take it slow. I'm going to make you scream for my cum."

Laughter shakes out of me. There's no way I'm screaming for anything when the casino is this quiet.

Then he pulls back his cock and massages his hand over my mound, dipping a finger inside my wetness. The shock runs through me as Jack's heavy breathing billows over my ear. He spreads me open with two fingers and my walls contract hard. The juice slides around his hand as he fucks me even though his cock is right there. It's right there!

"Please, Jack."

His chuckles cascade over my ears. "That's not *nearly* enough, sweetheart. You know what I want."

He wants the casino to echo with my screams. He wants security dashing up the staircase. He wants to feel like I can't live without him. I *know* I can't.

God. His fingers crash against a bed of nerves that shoot straight to my heart, making it fly. Again. And again.

"I'm going to come."

He slides out of me immediately, his tongue drawing a circle on my neck. "Good girl."

Both hands seize my tits, groping me in front of the entire casino as his laughter muffles in my hair. "You know you're not supposed to come without my permission."

My pussy tingles as he grabs my nipple and digs his fingernail into me. "Tell me you're *fucking* mine."

"I'm yours, Jack."

I've never been more aware of that than at this moment, half-naked, getting fingered above a casino.

My gasp hits the air as he slaps my tit.

"Not good enough."

He keeps sliding his dick along my clit, and it's like liquid heat rubbing against me, scratching an itch. I need the whole fucking length of him, throbbing inside me, like I need air.

"Give me your fucking cum!"

He bursts with laughter as my voice rings out clearly. There's no mistaking it. Several patrons turn their heads at the sound as Jack shakes behind me. I'm about to scream again, but he moves his cock ever so slightly. It rests right at my opening. His cock nudges me with an involuntary twitch and I let out a moan.

Then he spears into me, his thick cock filling me completely. He jerks my hips back and my moan rips through the air. His hand curls around my hair and pulls my head back, and then he brings his fingers to my face, still wet with my juice. I open my mouth as he slides them between my lips, and then I'm free to make all the noise I want against his palm.

"You little *slut.* You live for my cum, don't you?" His voice sounds strange, almost strangled.

I scream into his hand, the sound muffled as quick thrusts make me buckle against the railing.

"Tell me how much you want it."

The wonderful fullness disappears for a moment and my core clenches madly, missing him. I beg for more in his hand, and his pressure returns. He spreads me open, cock buried to the hilt. He pulses inside me, filling that deep ache.

"You feel that? That's me owning your pussy."

I push back against him. I want to fucking grind his cock, but he backs away from me.

"No, no, *no*," he chimes.

Another vicious slap burns my tattoo and he holds my hip with his other hand, giving me a few, quick, hard fucks. I've never been fucked so hard in my life. I can barely brace myself against the railing, and then he pulls out. I cry out as he slips his hand from my mouth and buries it in my hair.

His lips crush mine suddenly and a rush of emotion hits me. I want him. I love him—he pulls back, seething.

"You want a baby?"

"*Yes.*"

"You need to swallow first. There's more where that came from."

Jesus Christ.

I buckle to my knees as he pushes me down, still fisting my hair. His cock, slick with my pussy, bounces in my face. I grab him and swallow his head. He's so wide that my jaw hurts. Jack sucks in his breath when I force myself to take him all the way. His dick jumps inside my mouth, adding kerosene to the fire burning between my legs. My tongue sticks out, touching the very base of his cock.

"*Fuck.*"

I pull back, feeling his heartbeat pound through my lips as my tongue swirls around his head. The fist at the back of my head yanks me forward. I choke on his thickness as he ruts my mouth, the sounds of his groans pounding through me like the dick fucking my mouth. Then he tears at the roots of my hair, digging his fingers into my scalp.

Then his cock twitches in my mouth and salty liquid explodes at the back of my mouth. He holds my face there, my nose crushed against his abdomen.

"Oh *shit.*"

I swallow his cum down my throat, feeling more spurts coat my mouth as he pumps inside me, and then he pulls out, still hard. How the fuck is he still hard?

His hands clasp my arms and pull me upright so roughly that I fall against his chest. Then suddenly my arms fly to the railing again and he places a hand on my back, forcing me to bend. A pressure builds right behind my pulsing ache, and then he sinks right inside me like butter. Jack grabs both my hips and yanks me back using his hips like a fucking battering ram. His cock digs into me like a piston. Holy fuck. I've never been fucked like this before.

I cry out, but the breath is knocked out of me through the force of his thrusts. My arms buckle and collapse as he digs against me and pulls back. The agony and ecstasy reach a crescendo and I bite my arm. The wet sound of his hips slapping against me, his hands on my hips, his cock digging inside me—it's too fucking much. My throat tears with a scream as Jack makes a loud groan, holding me close as he comes for a second time. I clench over him as my body shakes from all the energy released. His cock pulses, swelling, and then I feel the jet of cum coating my pussy. I envision it seeping into my womb and striking a single egg. I glow at the thought of getting pregnant—and then finally getting to hold our baby in my arms. I want it with him. Only him.

He wraps a hand around my neck and pulls me upright, his dick still throbbing inside me. His lips find the spot right behind my ear and he whispers my name in a sigh that makes my skin flush with pleasure.

A pair of footsteps hurriedly making their way up the staircase startles us both.

"*Fuck.*"

He yanks down my blouse and skirt, and then he shoves his feet through his slacks, pulling them over his waist. I flatten my hair and clench my thighs together, feeling the slow trickle inside me.

Two men in security uniforms reach the staircase. "Sir, this is a *restricted area.*" One of them eyes our disheveled appearances and a frown deepens his sour face. "We're going to have to ask you to leave the casino."

Oh Jesus Christ.

"I just dropped thirty grand in your casino."

The guard stands in front of Jack, nostrils flaring. "Inappropriate behavior will not be tolerated—"

Jack stops him with a smirk as he slides his belt back on. Then he reaches inside his pocket and pulls out a couple hundred-dollar bills, tucking them in their shirt pockets.

I grab my purse and join Jack, stepping around the dumbfounded security guards as he loops his arm around my waist. He twists his head around and gives them a wink as we head downstairs. There's a crowd of people standing at the bottom of the staircase. A group of men erupt into cheers and slap Jack's back as he descends the stairs.

"Nice, man!"

"We enjoyed the show!"

I don't think my face could get any hotter than it is now. They actually saw us fucking. Oh my God.

Jack couldn't care less about the attention. He gives them a sarcastic wave and wheels me through the doors, where the cheers and laughter are finally drowned out.

"I'm so embarrassed, I could fucking die."

Jack lets out a bark of laughter. "Babe, what happens in Vegas *stays* in Vegas."

He links his hand through mine and gives me a quick kiss on my cheek. It's very fast, but his eyes linger, full of warmth. A sad smile tugs at the corners of his mouth. "Mike loved this place. We'd go together all the time."

Darkness clouds his face as my heart clenches painfully. The secret burns inside me like caustic acid. I want to tell him. I do, but then I think of my parents. Jack's wrath would rage through the MC, burning everyone alive in its path.

Jack's brow furrows as he walks down the street in silence, his fingers burning through my blouse.

* * *

The guilt builds. It banks into a fucking forest fire, consuming every spare thought. I'm so sick of myself that I can barely stand to look in the mirror. Weeks of waiting for him to come home and feeling my heart jump when he pulls me in for a kiss. Endless nights of being shattered in bed, clinging to his back, and forgetting my own name. Weeks of waiting for that goddamn stick to turn into two pink lines. So that I can finally tell him, and not feel like my guts are rotting inside out.

The door crashes open. It's past midnight—I can never sleep while he's out. A painful groan hits the air as Jack stumbles into the foyer, supported by one of Johnny's soldiers.

Oh my God.

His arm is in some sort of sling, but his feet drag behind him. The soldier, Ben, helps him to the couch.

"Jesus. What happened?"

Their chorus of, "Nothing," hits my ears, but I'm in no fucking mood to accept that. Not again.

"*What happened?*"

"He just got in a bit of trouble at a job."

"Again?"

I can't fucking believe this.

"Thanks, Ben." Jack glowers as he sinks into the couch cushions.

"What the fuck happened?"

He winces at the shrill sound of my voice, and Ben scurries out of sight. The front door shuts quietly and Jack snaps at me. "You know I can't talk about my work."

It's like an explosion. "Are you fucking serious? Is this how our conversations are going to go for the rest of our lives? I expect a fucking answer when you come home looking like this."

My emotions feel out of control, like a simmering pot of oil. It takes very little to set me off lately, and I don't know whether it's the stress of trying for a baby, his constant injuries, or the fact that I'm carrying something awful inside me.

His eyes widen at me, but my temper flares again.

"Johnny keeps sending you out on these dangerous jobs. I can't stand it!"

Suddenly his hand shoots out and he grabs my wrist, yanking me so that my face is inches from his. "You're way out of line, Beatrice. I can't fucking talk about it. That's for your sake as well as mine."

Doesn't he understand that seeing him like this hurts me? I can't stand seeing him injured. My eyes rapidly burn and flood over. It's Johnny's fault—I *know* it is. He hates Jack, and this is his way of punishing him.

He sighs, adopting a softer tone. "Stop crying, Beatrice. I'm *fine*."

I try to hold it in for his sake. A wave of self-loathing consumes me and I collapse into his chest, pressing my head against his wildly thumping heart. He touches his lips to my head and rubs my shoulder. It feels good, but my nerves are still jangling out of control.

"I couldn't drive home because of the painkillers they gave me. That's all."

I rip myself from him, agony twisting my guts when he gives me a wounded look.

"What the *hell* is the matter with you lately?"

Everything.

"I wasn't out on business. This was personal."

A swooping sensation gives me a sudden sick feeling. "Your brother?"

He gives me a sharp look. "Yes."

"And?"

He aims a violent kick at the coffee table leg. "And *nothing*! I've got fucking nothing!"

For a moment fear freezes my chest. Then he crumples with despair, holding his face in his hands. I suddenly wish I were the one being beaten up.

I run my hands through his hair, trying not to drown in the well of guilt.

JACK

My arm throbs like a son of a bitch, but I close my eyes and let the pain roll off my shoulders. Last night was a *fucking* nightmare.

Next to me, Sal wipes his head with his hand, a bead of perspiration on his upper lip. "I'm sorry, Jack."

"You warned me."

I sprained my shoulder lifting up one of those fat fucks who tried to rob me. Even after Ben and I took care of their bodies, I still had to empty a few chambers into that fat fucking asshole to vent my rage.

"It was a bad idea to go alone."

"Yeah, well, John's made it clear that he doesn't really give a flying fuck about finding out what happened."

Sal was the one who fed me the information. Some guys from the Popeyes MC claimed they heard about a made guy ordering a hit on someone in the family. He told me it was probably bullshit, but I couldn't stop myself from meeting them. And almost getting robbed by them.

Another dead end.

I grab the stiff drink poured in front of me, and I toss it down my throat.

"How's the marriage going?"

I shrug, somehow irritated by the question. "Not bad, actually."

"Really? You and the biker girl?"

The look of incredulity on Sal's face bothers me.

"She's a good wife." I make myself grin. "Turns out biker wives heel quite nicely."

"Are you fucking this broad?"

"Well, what else am I supposed to do with her?"

"*Tabarnak*. I don't think the MC will like that."

The MC can suck my dick.

There are too many guys sitting close to me to tell Sal the truth. She's not just a club daughter I'm banging. Sure, I wanted to fuck her the moment I met her, but it's much more than that. I live for watching those blue eyes light up when I come home, and the circle of her embrace. Now she's a person who I enjoy being around. Fuck, she makes me happy. Why is that so hard to admit?

"Speaking of your wife." Sal points across the room to Johnny's table.

A thin blonde woman sits across from my boss, her hands folded neatly in her lap.

What the fuck is she doing here? Why is she talking to my boss?

I set down my drink and immediately slide off the stool, making a beeline for my wife. My mood, always testy these days, is like a trail of fire leading to a barrel of gasoline. I can feel it racing forward.

The look on Johnny's face momentarily paralyzes me as I get close. He seems subdued. What the hell did she say to him? Beatrice jumps as I walk to her chair, sweeping my hand over her shoulder.

"What are you doing here?"

"She was looking for you." Johnny smirks at me as he plays with the ring on his finger. A sick, hot swoop of rage hits my abdomen as he meets my glare with a bored expression on his face. "Said it was urgent."

Her skin looks moist, as though she just stepped out of the shower and dressed herself in a hurry to meet me.

Johnny sits there, waiting for her to speak, but she stands up. Her blue eyes are so wide that I'm lost in them.

"I'll give you an hour, Jack."

"Fine."

She winces as I grab her upper arm and drag her out of the restaurant. "What the fuck do you think you're doing here?"

"I needed to see you!"

"You should never come here alone. I don't trust John."

We stand outside in the rapidly heating sunshine and I shove my hands in my pockets as I watch her stand there. She wears a small black camisole with no bra, because I can see her tits if I look down. Her hair is up in a loose, messy bun. The blonde tendrils and her wide eyes make her look so fragile—and beautiful. I really am lucky to have her. My hand slips underneath her jaw and I thumb her thick bottom lip.

"What is it, hon?"

"Not here."

The way she avoids my gaze gets me riled up. I don't like waiting, but her lips tremble and I don't want her making a scene out here. I take her arm and we enter my car.

"What is it, Beatrice?"

"Not here!"

She shakes and my heart splits in half when I hear that desperate sound coming from her chest.

"You'll tell me when we get home?"

I can only fucking guess what it is. The whole way back, she shakes with sobs and I take her hand in mine, trying every variation of, "Stop fucking crying," because it hurts me to see it. It hurts more than I ever could've imagined.

"*Tell me*. What the fuck is wrong?" I nearly scream at her. She's starting to freak me out.

I slam my brakes in front of my house and park as she slips out of the passenger seat and runs up the stairs, using her key to let herself in. Damn it.

I follow her, slamming the car door shut. Then I burst in my apartment and see her standing there, red tear streaks all over her face.

It tugs at my heart. I rush forward to gather her in my arms, but she shakes her head and backs away.

What the fuck?

"I have to tell you something I should have told you weeks ago." She spits it out bitterly and wraps her arms around herself.

"Why are you telling me now?"

"Because I'm pregnant."

Holy fuck.

It's as though the world turns on its head. I grasp for the nearest wall, suddenly dizzy. "You're sure?"

"I took a bunch of tests. They're all positive."

My heart thuds against my chest. If that's true, why does she look so miserable?

Jesus Christ, I'm going to be a dad.

Warmth delicately unfurls like petals from a flower. Beatrice cringes from my touch and acts as though the whole thing was a mistake.

"Why aren't you happy about this?"

"I am happy about the baby, but…" Her voice trails off and liquid blue eyes tentatively meet mine. "You'll never talk to me again."

"Whatever it is, I'm sure it's not that bad."

"It's about your brother!" she finally bursts out.

My mood shifts, skirting dangerously close to the well of rage I reserve for my brother. "What about him?"

Haunted eyes stare at me. "I saw what happened. I was there in the hospital."

"What?"

My hands shake.

"I didn't want to tell you because I was afraid."

"Tell me."

She opens and closes her mouth, and flinches when I yell at her.

"Fucking tell me, Beatrice!"

"I—I was in my cousin's room, right across from your brother's. I saw three men in leather cuts hanging outside the door. They went in and out. It was very fast." Her voice breaks and she doubles over, clutching her stomach. "I didn't know what happened! Then suddenly I heard people screaming for a code blue. I didn't put it together until we met. It was him, Jack!"

I grab her throat and pin her against the wall, waves of searing-hot rage licking up my sides. I want to bash this bitch into the wall. How fucking dare she?

"You knew all this time and never said a word?"

Her high gasp hits the air. "I wanted to tell you, but I was afraid of you."

I dig my fingers into her flesh. "You're fucking lucky that you're pregnant."

I'm no wife beater, but I'd like to give her a slap across the face.

"Jack, I'm sorry!"

I bite my lip, forcing myself not to scream. "What did the men look like? Did you recognize them?"

"N-no! I think they were f-from another MC, but it was dark and I couldn't see the pattern on the cut."

"God-fucking-dammit!" I plunge my fist through the drywall next to her head, and she screams. White powder explodes, and my knuckles bleed. Beatrice stumbles away from me, clutching her face.

"I'm sorry!"

"Think really fucking hard, Beatrice. There has to be something you remember. Some small detail that might help me."

She witnessed his murder and a part of me won't ever forgive her for keeping that secret from me, no matter what her intentions were. My heart rends in half. She lied to me for weeks.

Beatrice sits on the floor, her chest heaving. Tears fall silently down her cheeks as she stares at the tiles and shakes her head. "I can't remember anything significant, I'm sorry. They looked normal to me. I don't think they had any tattoos on their sleeves."

"No tattoos?"

She shakes her head and a lightning rod hits me, because how many patched members of an MC gang don't have tattoos on their sleeves?

"What else?" I bend down to her level, my heart hammering against my ribs as I search her face. I don't even care about the months of wasted time, I just want to know the truth.

"I just glimpsed them really quickly."

"*Think*, Beatrice."

"Wait—one of them might have had a small tattoo on his bicep."

My stomach tenses. "What?"

"A horn, I think."

Energy hits my chest. "A horn pointing down?"

"Yes, do you know what it means?"

Of course I know what it means. Every Italian knows that symbol. Jesus Christ. This proves beyond a shadow of a doubt that the family was involved.

I feel my insides caving in as if my guts vanished. My own brothers—the family I dedicated my fucking life to—betrayed me. It wasn't the MC. Johnny, that two-faced bastard who has been running me around all year on jobs without backup. But why?

She grasps my arm as I stand up, and my heart clenches painfully. Even she betrayed me.

"Jack, I'm so sorry. I wanted to tell you so many times."

"But you didn't."

Her touch on my skin is painful. Like a deep burn scorching away the muscle underneath. Her glittering eyelashes bat at me, and she looks down, stifling a hiccup of a sob.

She's not as innocent as she looks.

For a while she was the only light in my life. A candle flame, flickering that burned hotter as I woke up with her every day in my house. Now that's extinguished like everything else in my life.

Disgusted, I turn around. I head for the door, but then a thin arm wraps around my waist and a female body presses against my back. Every inch of her curves folds into my body. My chest tightens.

Fuck her.

I rip her hands from me and whirl her around, pinning her face against the wall. She cries out in discomfort as her cheek flattens, and I lean in, my voice trembling.

"When I come back, you're not going to be able to sit on your ass for a week."

I release her suddenly, hating the way my dick responds when her body is next to mine. I want to grab her hair in a ponytail and bend her over the kitchen table where I can see that tattoo burning right above her ass. I want to slap her around for the lies she told me. Lying by omission.

"I'll be back later."

"Jack, I—"

"Enough. I'm leaving."

She withers under my glare and shrinks away.

The pregnancy. My brother. All of it still implodes in my head. I see myself holding a newborn, and a deluge of panic suddenly swells inside me.

One fucking crisis at a time.

* * *

"Jack, get over here!"

I'm standing in the lobby of *Le Zinc*, slightly swaying on my feet with the aftermath of Beatrice's nuclear-bomb confession. François's voice snaps me to the present, and I look to see him standing in front of me, touching my shoulder.

"You all right?"

A sick feeling claws through my stomach. Who knows, he might have been one of the three sent to hold a pillow over my brother's face.

"Yeah, I'm fine."

"Johnny's going over the exchange later today."

Exchange. Drug deal. We use so many fucking code words to hide our true intentions. I wonder what phrase Johnny used when he ordered his men to take care of my paraplegic brother.

I follow him, weaving through the white-tablecloth covered tables to where that asshole sits, surrounded by his men. My throat is raw, as though I spent hours screaming. It would be so simple to just kill him right now. All I need to do is reach inside my jacket and aim. Fire.

Of course, I'd never make it out alive.

I examine them. Which one of them did it? I scan their bodies for the tattoo. Why does everyone have to wear suits all the goddamn time?

"Jack, sit down."

I'll fucking sit down after I rip your head off.

"What did your wife want?"

How did he do it? How does a man push aside every moral instinct to order a hit on a defenseless person, and not only that, but not have the fucking balls to take responsibility for it? He made them wear leather cuts. He wanted the police—everyone—to believe the MC was responsible. They weren't.

"*Jack.*"

Then I forget what the hell he asked me.

Johnny's lips crook into a grin.

"She's pregnant."

There's a moment of stunned silence and then their voices rise into laughter. It grates against my ears. I see myself reaching for necks and ripping them open with my bare hands.

"He knocked up the MC's daughter!"

"Hey, that makes two of us." Johnny's face cracks with a smile and he leans forward, grasping my shoulder. "Congratulations, Jack."

Congratulations.

The word slides over me like water on oil.

"I'm glad you took my advice and made her yours."

I didn't do it because you told me to, asshole.

The rest of them pat my back, and Sal gives me a look of concern. Whatever. The baby is far from my mind now. I want to find that fucking tattoo.

"We have a big arms deal with the Devils MC today. It's our first business deal since this alliance, so let's not fuck this up."

* * *

There's nothing but the distant, screeching sound of cars crumpling in on themselves. Piles of flattened multicolored metal surround us, insulating the noise. It's the same place I buried that piece of shit nurse, and I wonder what he looks like right now. If his bones were ground to dust.

I'm backup, merely standing in the background in case something gets fucked up. Johnny doubled the number of soldiers for this deal. I guess the two-timing prick doesn't trust the MC.

Crash or Flash or whatever his stupid name is stands in front of François, negotiating. His long brown beard twists around his head, flipping in the breeze whistling through the metal parts.

One of the men beside me rolls up his sleeves. The sun bakes the backs of our necks.

"Sounds good."

I catch the tail end of François's conversation with the biker. Adrenaline jolts through my veins and I whip my head when I see a flash, but it's just the sun reflecting off a car hood. Damn it. It's distracting. Hard to concentrate.

A crack splits the air and my jacket rips open at the shoulder, spraying blood.

I've been shot.

I barely register it before I dive under a heap of scrap metal. The outraged screams of my crew echo in the junkyard as a barrage of bullets smash into metal.

"CEASE FIRE!"

I whip around with my arm outstretched, gun aimed at that Crash motherfucker, but he holds up his hands, imploring us to stop. If it wasn't them, who the fuck was it? The gunshot came from their side.

There's movement to my right. The glare from a biker's gun. I barely see him, hidden in the heap of junk above me. He aims right at my face.

CRACK!

His head whips back as I fire a well-aimed shot, and I don't look to see him fall.

"What the FUCK!"

More gunshots thud in the heap I'm hiding behind, connecting sharply and glancing off. I'm going to fucking die hiding behind this thing.

A sear of pain slices down my neck, and liquid warmth blossoms over my skin. Fuck. At least it's shallow.

They're all above me. I aim a shot at another guy trying to take me out from above. I get him in the leg and he screams, then I pay attention to François, who blasts Crash's chest open with his shotgun.

I dive out from the scrap metal and launch myself toward the car as deadly zips thud into the ground. The scrape of a shoe—I clutch my gun and aim around the car, a hair trigger away from firing. Brian points his gun at me.

"Jesus!"

He takes a few seconds longer than me to lower his gun. I don't like the attitude on his face. We have no fucking time for it.

"What the fuck is going on?"

He ducks behind the car with me. "They set us up."

I glance once around the car, and a hole the size of my head blasts through the frame. Jesus. Blood trickles down and I think of her hair, tickling my neck. Beatrice. She's alone at the house. All the things I said. Why did I have to be such an asshole? Why didn't I tell her that having her around saved my life?

My shoulder throbs and the wound on my throat bleeds freely. The windshield shatters and bullets pepper the interior as Brian hurls himself over the hood and fires.

Fuck this. We're going to die.

Brain is blasted off his feet and lands on his back, his mouth exploding with color. Fuck! I rush to his side as a dark hole made in his jacket slowly smokes. He coughs up bright-red blood and his eyes roll back.

Jesus *fuck*.

I take the knife strapped to my ankle and I cut away his jacket and shirt, immediately covering the dark hole in his chest with my palm.

"Come on, you fuck!"

Goddamn it, he got shot in his arm, too. I cut away the jacket completely and roll up his sleeve.

And that fucking *cornicello* stares at me, right where she said it would be. Shock slowly runs through my body as Brian wheezes for air next to me. His limp hand searches for me. He was one of them. My body burns with white-hot rage.

I dig my thumb into his bullet wound and he opens his red-stained mouth in a wordless, bubbly cry.

"You piece of shit."

"J-Jack! I can't breathe!"

His lungs make a horrible wheezing sound. Fuck, I couldn't ask for a better setup.

"You killed him, didn't you? Who gave the order?"

But he can't talk. He just inhales, making that rattling sound. Then I just reach over and pinch his nostrils shut. Brian tries to breathe through his mouth, but there's too much blood. He weakly grasps my hand and bloodshot eyes beg me for forgiveness as I choke off his air supply.

Drowning in your own blood must fucking suck.

Blood-filled bubbles expel from Brian's mouth. He gasps, the blood gurgling in his throat. Blue tinges his lips and capillaries burst in his eyes.

It must be excruciating.

I relish in it.

His eyes seem to glaze over and his fingers loosen around me. Then Brian's hand finally thuds to the ground, limp.

Rot in hell.

This is perfect. Clean. If only I could wipe the panic away.

"JACK!"

One down. Three to go.

A hand violently grabs my arm, and suddenly François's face swims in front of me. "What the fuck is wrong with you? I'm calling your name!"

Pops of gunfire crack through the air, one at a time, followed by heavy thuds. I look around the car to see the rest of the crew picking off the bikers one by one.

"Brian!" he drops down to the body and shakes his frozen shoulder.

"He's dead."

The temporary relief falls as my neck singes with pain. My head churns as I look at the carnage in the junkyard.

* * *

The lean boss sits behind the desk, a pulse bumping in his forehead as we wait for the inevitable explosion.

Then he slams his fist into the wood, knocking over a picture frame.

"What the fuck happened? How did you manage to fuck this up so badly?"

I finger the patch on my neck, turning over everything in my head. "They shot first. Their guy aimed a gun right at me. That's how I got this." I point toward my shoulder.

"It was a setup," François agrees.

"What the fuck?"

Johnny sinks back into his chair, brow furrowed in disbelief.

"They killed Brian."

No, I did.

"Goddamn it—motherless fucks—*putain de merde*. They're all fucking dead! We're finished. We're done with the Devils." He rises to his feet as his face turns beet red. "I tried to end this shit! I gave them another fucking chance because I was sick of our guys getting hurt for no fucking reason, and they fucking spat in my face."

Something bothers me about it. "I don't know."

He whips his head at me. "What don't you know?"

"It seemed too sloppy. They were going to lure us there? For what? And why send their worst guns and no backup?"

"You said he aimed the gun right at you."

"I know what I saw," I snap. "I just think there's more to this."

Johnny shakes it off, baring his teeth. "I want them *all* dead. They wanted a war, and I'm going to give them one."

Sal leans across the desk. "Frankly I agree with Johnny. They've done nothing but disrespect us since we've made this alliance."

"I'm going to blow that fucking compound to kingdom come."

Jesus.

"John—it's a bad fucking idea."

"Who asked your opinion?"

Underneath my skin I smolder. He's one of them. I know he is. But how am I supposed to get to him?

"Your wife has family there. So does mine."

He wrinkles his nose. "Since when do you give a shit about bikers?"

Since I married and fell for one of them.

"Do we really need more heat from the CSIS? The Trudeau heist wasn't enough?"

Finally the guys murmur in agreement.

Why the fuck am I giving advice to this piece of shit?

He sits on his desk and runs his hands through his hair. "All right, everyone get out. Not you, Jack."

Fuck.

The door to his office closes behind the last man and I wonder how Johnny's brains would look splattered on the wall behind him. He crosses his arms and eye-fucks me.

"You need to divorce that girl."

Well, that's not what I expected.

"What?"

"You've got to get rid of her."

I slowly rise from my chair as fire hot enough to burn my clothes radiates off my body. "No."

He narrows his eyes. "The alliance is over. You realize that the first thing she'll do is head over to the police station and tell them she was coerced into a marriage with you, right?"

Never.

I stop an inch from Johnny's face. "She's my wife and she's going to stay that way. Not you or anyone is going to convince me otherwise."

A widened look crosses Johnny's face until he lets out a small laugh. "You're a fucking idiot, Jack."

Don't punch him. You can't do this here in front of everyone.

"Fuck you."

"You sure you want to take that tone with me?"

"She's mine. I'm not giving her back."

I can't stand another moment in his presence. Slimy *fuck*. I turn my back on John and wrench open the door, slamming it behind me. Who the fuck does he think he is?

"Jack, wait!"

"What?"

Sal grabs my arm as I storm out of Johnny's office, pulling me near the exit door in the kitchens. His face is tense and he won't let go of my arm.

"What did he want with you?"

"He wanted to talk to me about my wife. He wants me to divorce her."

Fucking idiot.

"Are you?"

"No!"

"Why the fuck not, Jack? She's a liability."

"I don't care," I snarl. "She's pregnant with my kid. I'm not throwing her to the streets or giving her back to those fucking deranged lunatics."

Sal's face is ashen and a thread of anxiety unspools.

"What?"

"John's not going to let this go. In his mind, your wife is going to put you in jail the moment she has the chance. You, Johnny, who knows how many others. All she has to do is run to the CSIS and they'll give her a new identity."

I slam my fist on the stainless steel counter. "She's not going to do that."

She had my name tattooed on her ass, for Christ's sake.

"Doesn't matter what you think. He's going to take care of her, one way or the other."

Take care of her?

An icy feeling spreads through my veins.

Like Mike?

Oh God.

"He wouldn't."

Pleading brown eyes meet mine. "You think he gives a fuck? Get her out of town today."

"Thanks, Sal."

I throw my shoulder into the exit door, nausea rising up my throat. My wife and baby are at risk. He's right. She can't stay here, not when I'm being shot at and I don't even know who to trust anymore.

My lungs crush like crumpled wings and I fight to draw breath at the thought of her leaving me. I never stopped to think of how much I needed her.

It won't be forever.

BEATRICE

Wine-red walls rise to a ceiling with intricate crown molding. I stare at all the rich details, the abstract art hanging on the walls, as Maya's baby climbs over me and babbles happily.

Maya sits beside me in her long skirt, waving at her baby.

"I'm really glad you picked me up, but won't Johnny be getting home soon?"

She shakes her head and lets out an exasperated sigh. "He's being an ass." Her eyes roll over to me. "How's Jack?"

Also being an ass.

Pain makes a sharp dent in my happiness as I think of the ugly things he said right before he left. He was furious and rightly so, but it still hurt like hell.

"I just found out we're having a baby."

Maya's high gasp hits my ears painfully. "Congratulations!"

"Thanks."

Matteo sits on my stomach and gives me a toothless grin that makes my heart melt.

"Can I take him home with me?"

She laughs and plucks Matteo from my body. "Yeah, maybe when we have a date night." She shakes her head. "I can't believe you're fucking pregnant! Oops!" She hastily covers her baby's ears.

"I didn't think I would ever be accepted by the family until I had his kids."

"They'll accept you or they'll get their teeth knocked out."

Somehow I doubt Jack will ever knock someone's teeth out for me. "It's never going to happen."

"Hey, I saw what your husband did to those guys at the party. He loves you, Bea. Otherwise he wouldn't have gone to bat for you."

Hope flutters in my chest. "You think so?"

BAM!

We scream as the door flies open and Johnny's tall silhouette appears between the walls. He walks in, slamming the door shut, and stops at the sight of me.

My heart slams against my chest.

"What the hell is she doing here?"

Maya stands up, her eyes widening with surprise at the growl in his voice. She sets Matteo down at my feet.

"Don't talk to me like that. She's my cousin and I'll bring her over if I want."

Johnny turns toward his wife, his features thick with rage. "You brought her? Why the fuck—"

"She's my cousin," Maya says, louder than ever.

"I know," he begins with waning patience, "but she's also a fucking biker who was coerced into a marriage with one of my men."

"I trust her."

He smirks, folding his arms. "Well, I don't."

"I'm your wife and my trust should be good enough for you. I've known her my whole life, not you! I decide who I want to see, not you!"

Matteo's cry suddenly breaks the sound of his parents fighting. I pick him up as tears bead in his eyes and I rub his back until the cries subside. Johnny's taut face loosens somewhat.

"Sweetheart, you have no idea what's going on right now. We're at war. I don't give a fuck if she's Pope Francis, I don't trust her."

He grabs his wife's shoulders and gives her a kiss on her furious face. Then he stops in front of me. Matteo outstretches his tiny arms. "Papa!"

Even though I fucking hate him, I have to admit that he loves his son. Johnny gently takes him from my arms and holds his son to his chest, kissing the baby's head over and over as if to reassure himself.

Dark, restless eyes settle on me. "I'm just trying to protect my family."

Annoyance bristles in my chest.

"She's married to one of your soldiers."

"I don't care, sweetheart. Right now, I trust no one." Then he turns back to me. "I'll call your husband to come get you."

Johnny stalks off with the baby in his arms and Maya fumes after him. I sink into an armchair, depressed.

"He won't stop me from visiting you. I don't give a shit what he says."

"Maybe when my kid is born, he'll change his mind."

We spend the rest of the time chatting, and then Johnny reenters the room with the baby snug in his arms when there's a knock at the door. Maya answers.

Jack stumbles into the house, and the first thing I notice is that there's a bandage on his neck and a large tear in his suit.

"What happened to you?"

He gives a quick glance at John, suddenly looking terrified. "Let's go. We're going home."

Maya gives me a sad smile as Jack grabs my hand and pulls me out of the living room, but Johnny does nothing but give me a cool, appraising nod.

He slams the door shut, cutting off Maya's good-bye when we leave the house, and I wring my hand out of his. "What the fuck is your problem?"

A vicious look snarls over Jack's face. "You have no idea what just happened. Get in the car, Beatrice. I'm not messing around."

Fine.

I slide into the passenger seat and Jack immediately starts the engine, peeling out of Johnny's driveway and down the street. The sheer desperation in Jack's eyes stops me from making a nasty remark.

"What happened?"

"I can't think— I can't. Everything's just fucking out of control."

I've never seen him like this. Jesus, he looks *scared.* Fear's not an emotion I like to see on my husband's face.

"Just let me think."

I don't say a word until we get home, and the moment we step through the door Jack pulls me into his bone-cracking embrace. I flatten against his chest, hearing his heartbeat pound against my ear like a heavy drum. The floodgates open as a rush of emotion fills me. "Jack, I'm sorry for what I did—"

"Don't, it doesn't matter anymore." He pulls back and holds my face, his thumbs caressing my skin. Devastation slams into him—he looks like he's experienced a hundred years of misery.

"Beatrice, I love you."

The air disappears.

"You make me happy, and now we have this blessing inside you. I thought that we had a chance, but we don't."

My eyes sting with tears. "What? Are you—" *Are you breaking up with me?*

"You have to go."

My feelings, soaring high, crash back down. "Go?"

"It's not safe for you here. We're at war with the Devils again. I almost got killed today, and John wants you gone from my life."

"I'll stay," I choke out in tears. "I don't care how dangerous it is."

"I care," he says, tenderness creeping inside his voice.

He loves me.

"Beatrice, you're all I have now. Everyone else is gone."

"But I don't understand! Why does Johnny care about me?"

"He doesn't trust you. He thinks you're going to rat me out now that the alliance is over."

"I would never do that!" I yell into his apartment. "Never!"

A smile tugs at his mouth. "He'll never believe us."

"What's he going to do, kill me? I'm carrying your child."

Pity fills Jack's gaze. "He doesn't care about some knocked-up biker girl, even if you are my wife. He killed my brother, Beatrice."

The breath catches in my throat. "No, I don't believe it!"

I don't want to believe it.

"Baby, who else would've ordered a bunch of Italians to dress up in leather cuts and kill my brother? It had to come from him."

Tears spill over my lids as I look at him. My heart swells and I clutch at Jack's chest. "What about our baby?"

He flinches as if he was struck in the face.

"Jack, I love you!"

"I know."

He bends down and crushes his lips against mine, silencing my cries. A well of desire quickly ramps up as his hands slide down my body, stroking my curves as though he wants to imprint them in his brain. He grabs my arms, steering me backward toward our bedroom. Even when he's vulnerable, he can't help but push me around. It was in his nature to break me just as it was my nature to submit to him. I never craved anyone's touch like his.

My legs hit the back of the bed and I fall, landing softly on the mattress. Jack rips his jacket off and throws it in a corner, and then I see his ripped dress shirt and the bandage around his shoulder, already damp with blood. He ignores my gasp and his body climbs over mine, his lips feverish. He breaks away, his face flushed.

"Fuck, I don't have enough time to take you the way you were meant to be taken."

I just want this moment to last forever, while we're still clinging to each other. Happy and whole.

Don't make me go.

He rolls my shirt off my head and my skin prickles with desire as his starved gaze falls over my curves. "You are unbelievably sexy."

No one's ever made me feel so amazing. I keep imagining myself alone in a lonely apartment, singing to a baby in a cradle. My eyes sting with tears and Jack blurs in my vision.

He sinks down and palms my cheek, lowering himself to give me a kiss that makes my skin flame. "I'll come back for you."

I can't trust myself to say anything without bursting into tears, so I just nod.

"I promise."

Another tender kiss falls on my lips, and I wrap my hand around his neck, pulling him down. He reaches behind my back and unclasps my bra. A tingle runs through my pussy as his hand envelops my breast. He swallows my gasp, deepening the kiss. Then I feel his hard cock digging into my leg, and a thrill hits my core.

He breaks from the kiss, and I'm dizzy. "I want you."

He grins and thumbs my bottom lip. "Yeah, you're always so hungry for cock."

I love him—love the dirty shit he says. "I wanted you the moment you told me to kiss you."

The sound of him ripping off his slacks makes my pussy throb with a sudden ache. I help him push them off, running my hands over his strong hips. A smile staggers over his face.

"I know, baby. You were practically screaming for a man like me. Girl like that—sitting alone in a bar looking so lost. I couldn't stay away."

He was so possessive, even when he wasn't thrilled to marry me. I fell for him hard, but his was a slower build.

Jack grabs the waistband of my skirt and tugs. The black skirt pulls to my knees and he pushes me to my side, spreading his hand over my ass.

A chuckle escapes his throat. "I mean, look at this. *Property of Jack.* You really are a piece of work, sweetheart."

I grab his neck and pull him toward me. "It's not a joke. Women in the MC get tattoos like this all the time."

His face spreads into a wide, handsome smile that takes my breath away. "I'm not laughing." He seals his lips against mine, biting my lower lip. "But they probably don't get them tattooed on their ass, do they?"

"I thought you'd like to see it there."

He smacks my ass, making a loud cracking sound. "I love it."

He strokes the burn for a moment and then flips me to my back, parting my legs as his huge cock swings in front of me. A bead of pre-cum rolls down his cock and falls on my thigh. He runs his hands down my legs.

"I'm sorry." His face stretches into a primal grin. "I'm trying to be sweet for you, but I can't fucking do it."

I sit upright as desire pulses through me. I bury my hand in his hair and scrape his scalp with my fingers. "I don't want sweet. I want you."

His breath blows hot air over my lips for a moment. Then he buries his hand in my hair, pulling it until it hurts. His tongue hits my nipple like the cool edge of a knife. A surge rushes through my pussy as he closes his hot mouth, swirling around my nipple. Then he bites down hard, enough to make me try to twist out of him.

"Fuck!"

He laughs slightly as he pulls back from the deep-red mark, sweeping his thumb across it admiringly. "I'm going to leave you with marks all over your fucking body, so that every time you look at yourself you'll see me, claiming you as mine. They'll take weeks to fade."

Weeks without him?

He tongues my breast, sucking me into his mouth until it burns. Another fucking mark. Then I feel a pressure between my legs and I see his veiny, thick cock sinking into me. Jesus. It's like coming home after a long day. It just feels so fucking good.

The pain bites through the pleasure as he gives me another mark with his teeth, bruising my flesh. At the same time his thickness spreads me open, gliding up my walls to anchor hard inside me.

It fills me up completely, temporarily satisfying that ache burning inside me. A gasp trembles from my lips as his wet mouth slides across my skin. Another burst of pain makes me arch my back, but then his hips dig into me and electricity numbs out the pain.

He pulls back, his dark hair hanging around his face as he surveys the marks all over my tits. A primal grin tugs at his lips and he makes a low growl in his throat, hammering my pussy hard.

All the love is gone from his eyes, washed out by his instinct to claim me.

"Does my cock feel good?"

"Yes! Don't stop!"

His arms wrap around me tight and my eyes roll as he rams his hips. Air knocks from my chest with his thrusts, leaving me gasping. Holy fuck.

Another sharp pain hits my flesh, this time on my unmarked breast. He soothes it immediately, circling his tongue around my nipple and sucking hard—delivering a jolt of pleasure to my core.

Panting, he moves himself away from me, his cock slipping out. Then his rough hands seize my hips and flip me over so that I'm on all fours. A vicious slap hits my right cheek right before his thighs press against mine and that delicious pressure spears through me.

"You're mine."

My screams reverberate through the apartment as he pulls me against him, cock hammering my tight cunt until I feel myself falling apart. His weight bears on me and I fall forward, catching myself by my elbows. He pounds me into the mattress, his hand sneaking underneath my body to cup my swollen breast. My screams punctuate the sounds of his groans and his balls slapping against my pussy.

His body undulates like a wave, shoving me toward the wall. My palms flatten against it, my arms absorbing the shock of his thrusts. He kisses my neck, his frantic breathing billowing over my damp skin.

"Come, baby. Come for me."

A violent tremor rocks through my body as I clench myself and push against his hips, feeling the gush of liquid as he jerks against me.

His weight sags over me as his cock ruts me deep, filling my womb with his cum. My head turns with his finger and he kisses me long and hard, his tongue sweeping inside my mouth. Exhausted, my body melts into a pool as shocks of pleasure hit my heart.

He takes me in his arms and rolls over. Smooth hands glide over my skin, pulling me close as I nestle my head right under his, inhaling his masculine scent.

He won't be a room away anymore. I won't be able to fuck him, feel his heart thrumming against my ear like it is now. I'll just be alone.

* * *

A blaring cacophony of honking horns doesn't penetrate the solitude I've created in this car. Their high beams flash behind us, but Jack ignores them pointedly. His strong hand grips mine, his thumb caressing my skin.

I don't want to go.

I don't want to step outside this car and leave him, but my eyes refuse to make tears. I won't make this harder on him.

"How long do you think I'll have to stay away?"

"I don't know."

What if he never calls for me? What if he has to miss the birth of his child?

"I just know that I need to protect my family. This is the only way I know how."

A smoldering feeling burns at my grief. I stamp it under my feet. "I understand."

Then time freezes. Someone's waiting for the other to say good-bye. Jack cracks first, leaning over to plant a kiss on my cheek. It's so dry. Devoid of passion. But then he lingers there, stroking my cheek.

"I love you."

I look away from the affection shining in his eyes. "I love you, too."

"This isn't good-bye, Beatrice. I'll see you soon."

"Okay."

I unbuckle my seatbelt and he springs out of his car to help get the luggage out of the trunk. With a great sigh I open the door and step out into the bright sunshine.

People walk quickly to and from the metro station as rush hour casts its orange gaze over the streets. Jack lifts my suitcase out of the car. A white bandage still sticks on his neck, hiding his latest brush with death.

A petrifying feeling slowly freezes my body. How the fuck can we do this? The MC is after him, and the mob is full of rats. How long before one of them gets him? The goal seems insurmountable—impossible. Maybe he could've handled one of the crises. But two at once?

This might be the last time I see him alive.

The roll of my suitcase cuts away my thoughts as Jack slides a comforting arm around my waist.

"I guess this is good-bye for now."

I can't take it.

I curl into his arms and seize his waist, looking up at him but not finding the words. What am I supposed to say? Good luck? What I really want to do is beg him to come with me, to plead with him to stay alive. *Stay the fuck alive.*

"Jack, I'm scared."

His hand tightens around my waist. "Just board a train and go. Get the hell out of here. You'll be fine."

I'm not scared for myself.

"What about you?"

He lifts an eyebrow. "I can take care of myself. Don't worry about me. You're the one carrying something special."

His hand momentarily brushes over my stomach and I hold him there, thinking of the tiny life growing inside me. Fuck, I forgot I was pregnant on top of everything else.

"I'll do everything I can to bring our family back together, but you have to promise me something." He grabs both my shoulders and digs into my bones. "Don't come back here. No matter what you might hear, you have to promise me you'll stay away until I call you."

Never come back?

A tremor creeps into my voice. "What if something happens to you?"

"Not even then. Beatrice, promise me."

I can't do it. The carefully constructed wall I built around me starts to topple. It's too much.

"I can't do that!"

The grip on my shoulders is painful. "You have to. For both our sakes."

I squeeze his middle, unable to bear the moment when I'll have to tear myself away. "But—"

"Promise me!"

A glint of desperation fractures his eyes.

"I—I promise."

"Good girl."

My body bumps his chest as he pulls me in, slowly squeezing air out of me.

"I love you, baby. I'll come back for you soon."

I don't know what to tell him. The words won't come. Nothing will dispel the torment raging inside, so I just let him hug me.

"Go, Beatrice. We've been here too long."

"Okay."

We break away and he shoves his hands deep in his pockets.

"Bye."

"Safe trip, Beatrice."

A crooked smile tugs at his lips as he gives me a wink, and I turn around, forcing my legs to walk. It's as though they're filled with lead, because this doesn't feel right. Everything inside me screams to run back into Jack's arms. I walk across the pavement to the pay stations. A glance over my shoulder. He's still there, watching me with that sweet smile. I never thought he'd be gentle with me. I turn around.

A loud crack makes me duck and a large spark explodes over the metal ticket dispenser. What the hell? Did it short-circuit? A man's voice screams behind me, and I turn around violently. A sharp, intense pain slices my hip. I feel it like a searing-hot brand sizzling my skin, and then I see Jack ducked behind his car door, his arm extended.

CRACK. CRACK.

The ground explodes a foot away from where I'm standing and Jack screams over the noise.

"BEATRICE, RUN!"

I get up and leave my suitcase behind, barreling past the ticket machines into the station. A wet feeling at my hip distracts me, and I look down.

A wave of dizziness strikes my head and I brace my palm on the wall.

Blood.

Dark red spreads over my pink t-shirt. Then the pain starts to throb sharply. Oh God, I don't want to look. My brain can't process what's happening. All of it is like the striking visuals of an action movie. Jack, firing his gun in the middle of broad daylight. The explosions and sparks at my feet. The blood spreading over my hip.

Am I shot?

"He's got a gun!"

I look up, heart racing, and I see Jack sprinting toward me. He bellows like a wounded animal when he sees the wound at my side.

"Jack, what's going on?"

I'm surprised at the calm in my voice.

He ignores my question and lifts my shirt. I feel the fabric unsticking from my wound. "You got grazed. You'll be fine," he says in a quick, hurried voice.

He yanks me to my feet so quickly that I have vertigo. "We need to get the fuck out of here before the cops get here. Come on."

Numbly I follow Jack back outside, noticing the crowd of huddled people. There's a body near Jack's car. My horrified gasp catches Jack's attention.

"Come on!"

He opens the car door and yanks me inside. I don't feel like any of this is actually happening to me. It's too bizarre—must be a dream. I hiss in pain when I try to sit up. Jack's head snaps to me, anguish all over his face. Feelings return and I realize how fast I'm breathing. The sound is sharp in the car. Fear trickles in as he starts the car and guns the engine.

"*They shot me.*"

"THAT SON OF A BITCH!"

I jump in my seat as he beats the dashboard with his fist. The radio screen smashes and pieces of plastic stick into his knuckles.

"JOHNNY!" he screams, spittle flying from his mouth. "He sent those guys after us. He wants us fucking gone, so I'm going to fucking kill him."

It's all confused. I can't think straight as Jack drives like a maniac down the streets and flies through downtown Montreal. He screeches to a halt outside a bar, and then within seconds he's dragging me out of the passenger seat.

"What are you— Where are we going?"

"I've got to leave you here."

"Leave me? Are you fucking kidding?" My voice rises to a shriek in the sidewalk as he drags me by my arm.

"I've got to end this. I've got to get rid of him."

Patrons in the bar stare as we burst through the door. They swing their heads around and Jack drags me to the back rooms, where Sal sits at a table, counting stacks of money. Two other guys hang nearby.

He looks up. "Jack—Beatrice! What the fuck happened?"

"Johnny happened!"

Jack's voice trembles the ceiling as he releases my arm.

"He went after her—both of us! He's fucking dead, Sal. I'm finding him and I'm putting an end to this bullshit!"

Sal rises to his feet. "Jesus Christ, Jack. Have you lost your fucking mind?"

My heart races as he rounds on Sal, fists raised. "He sent Ricardo and Ben after me—I KNOW HE DID. I'm done. He's dead. He came after my wife!"

Without waiting for Sal to speak, he turns to me. I flinch when he grabs my shoulders.

"Stay fucking put. Do not leave Sal's sight."

Sal raises a beefy arm. "Jack, we need to talk to the other bosses—the commission—"

Muscles rippling, Jack seizes an empty bottle of wine from the table and smashes it against the wall, shattering it into thousands of pieces. Then he takes the jagged neck and grabs the closest man, digging the broken glass into his neck.

"Jack!"

"If you lay a hand on my wife, I'll rip open your insides while you're still alive."

"Jesus, Jack!"

Then he flings the broken glass to the floor and gives Sal a cold glare. "Watch her."

JACK

The streetlights bleed into the darkness the longer I keep my eyes open. Then I blink and a glaze sharpens everything into focus again. The car screams as the lights flash a bright green.

Go kill John.

I can't hear anything but the roar of my blood and my own voice screaming in my head.

It was John this whole time. He's a fucking cancer in my life, and now he's attacking people that he has no right to touch. What the hell ever happened to *omertà*? That bastard held on to that code tighter than most guys hold on to their balls. We're not supposed to touch family. Wives are off limits—and he just tried to kill her in broad daylight.

Is he sending a message to me? That he's boss and can do whatever the fuck he wants?

Message read, loud and clear. You're fucking dead, Johnny.

I race down the streets of Montreal like a madman. Murderous rage builds inside me like a crescendo. Fuck, this is so easy. I should have done this weeks ago. I park my car a couple blocks down from John's house and I move quickly through shadows. Heat pounds through my limbs as I grab my gun at my side, and I raise my fist. The wood rattles as I pound the door.

Amazingly it opens a few moments later and Johnny's wife stands in front of me. Fuck. I would rather not do this in front of her.

Her eyebrows knit in concern. "Jack, what's wrong?"

"Where is your husband?"

Nothing but red flies in front of my vision as she mumbles something. I won't be delayed any longer. My brother waited months for justice. I push her aside, batting her away.

"Jesus!"

"I need to see him."

An extremely offended look crosses her pretty face as she shuts the door. "He's in his study."

Perfect.

I let his wife lead me to her husband, the effort of keeping myself from drawing my gun shaking my limbs. She'll lead me to his slaughter, and after that… After that, I'm not sure.

My mind is clear the moment she opens the door and John lifts his head. Calm hatred fills me with bloodlust when he says something and I step inside. The door closes, trapping us both.

"Jack. What brings you here?"

How can the bastard pretend not to know? His relaxed posture betrays nothing as he bends over sheaves of paper. As I sit down I swing my hand from my jacket. The gun flashes in the overhead light and Johnny spots it, but too late. His hand reaches under his desk and I point the gun square at his chest.

"Hands on your fucking head."

Johnny freezes, his gaze filled with cold rage. "What are you doing?"

"Do as I say, or I'll blow a hole in your chest."

The air feels thick and my voice trembles like it's on the verge of explosion.

Even though that bastard knows I'm not fucking around, he refuses to weaken in front of me. Slowly he raises his hands on his perfectly styled hair. An impassive expression falls on his face. It says: *Fine, kill me, but you won't last a day after I'm dead.*

This is it. All I have to do is pull the trigger, and Johnny's no longer boss. He's no longer anything.

A flicker of something glints in his eyes when I raise the gun to his head.

"Why did you do it?"

"Do what?"

A burst of emotion rises up my throat and I slam my fist on the table. The gun rattles in my hand. "You know what you fucking did, so don't try to deny it!"

Johnny's voice stays even. "I have no idea what you're talking about."

"MY BROTHER! MY WIFE!" Corrosive hatred rises inside me as confusion and anger cloud his face. I want him to admit it. "You tried to have them killed, and I'm fucking done playing your games!"

"I don't know who is feeding you this information, but it's false."

"BULLSHIT! I was at the train station with her, you piece of shit! Your guys went after her."

"Why the fuck would I want to kill your wife?"

My eyes burn as a vision of Mike's broken body haunts me. "Because she's a loose end! Because that's what you do! Sal can back me up—you hired Brian and two other men to take care of my brother—"

"*I did not kill your brother.*"

"DON'T FUCKING LIE TO ME!"

"If I wanted him dead, I wouldn't have been so sloppy. I'm no fucking coward—I wouldn't make them wear leather cuts."

No, I won't let him do this. He's just trying to manipulate me.

"And your wife? Why the fuck would I do that in the middle of broad daylight? Despite what you might think of me, I would never touch another man's family."

I refuse to let the nuggets of truth sink in, but everything's confused now.

"Why the fuck would I want to jeopardize this alliance? It makes no sense, Jack."

"To fuck with me! All year you've been sending me on these fucking jobs and I risked my goddamned *life*."

"What jobs?" he roars. "What the fuck are you talking about?"

"Damn you," I say in a tight voice, gun trembling. "You know what I'm talking about. The jobs Sal called me for that were directly from you."

He lowers his hands from his head, the blood drained from his face. He looks like a pale shadow of his former self. "Jack," he says, pitying me. "He's playing you."

What?

And the energy saps out of my limbs.

"Isn't it fucking obvious? He wants me dead, and he fed you shit all year to get you to do this."

Horror makes the rage dart out of sight like quick, silver fish. The gun lowers from his head.

"Why? Why would he?"

"He probably killed your brother—made them dress in leather cuts to throw off the cops, but made it obvious that they weren't MC to us so that you'd suspect me."

"Why the fuck would he do that?"

A grim smile stretches Johnny's mouth. "To start a war? To take my place? Who the fuck knows."

Sal knew I would run over to Johnny the moment my wife was threatened, so he had them attack her.

Then I drop the gun as panic blooms in my chest.

Oh my God, I left her with him!

Suddenly the cold barrel of a gun stares into my eyes as John stands up, his demeanor as icy as the metal pressed against my forehead.

His voice cracks, his hand shaking somewhat as he holds the gun to my head.

"No one's *ever* gotten this close to ending my life."

"John, *come on.* We're on the same side here—"

"I'll let you live long enough to leave Montreal."

Everything's different now. I need his help.

"Please, John. I left her with him." Regret pounds between my ribs as I choke on my next words. "She's pregnant with my kid—and you—" Then my voice cracks with outrage. "You owe me!"

"You put a gun to my head not five minutes ago."

A ripple of anger runs through me. "Can you fucking blame me? You did fuck all to find out who killed Mike."

He grits his teeth. "I was busy trying to keep anyone else from being killed! That's what this whole alliance was about, and now it's gone to fucking hell!"

"John, I don't fucking care. Beatrice is at that bar with Sal. I told her to trust him."

It's like a bottomless pit just opened beneath my feet.

He blows out his cheeks. "Where exactly?"

"At the Whale and Ale."

"Let's go."

Tension rides my limbs as we burst out of the office. His wife swoops on John the moment we leave.

"What's going on in there?"

"We've got to go deal with something. Maya, don't answer the door or accept any calls from anyone but me."

She blanches. "Why?"

"I can't get into it."

Beatrice is waiting for us.

"Let's go!" I scream, nerves frayed.

I disregard the withering look thrown my way. My stomach is tied in knots over the colossal mistake I made. I trusted a man who used me like a gun.

The balmy night feels suffocating, like a heavy fog settling deep in my lungs so that I can't exhale.

"We'll take my car."

I rip open the passenger door of his BMW and slide into the seat as Johnny sits beside me, slamming his door shut.

"I hope you realize this doesn't change shit between us," Johnny says as he starts his car. "How many fucking times did I tell you I had nothing to do with Mike's murder?"

My chest swells as we peel out of his driveway. "You need me to clean up house. Sal's a fucking parasite. I cannot believe I actually looked up to that man."

Yellow light flashes over Johnny's face. "What did he say when he'd send you on these jobs?"

"He said they were requests from you. That if I wanted to get back in your good graces, I would do them and shut my mouth."

"Jesus FUCKING Christ! Ten fucking years I've been working with this guy, and now I have to make an example out of him."

"All due respect, John, but he's mine."

"Fuck you. I'm the boss."

"If you're right, he murdered my brother."

Silence swallows the echo of pain in hungry gaps. Johnny turns his head toward me slowly.

"He may have killed your brother, but—"

"—But nothing! I have the right to put a bullet in his fucking head."

"I need him alive."

Fucking bullshit.

"I need to know how big of a rat he is, and I need to be sure."

"How are you not sure?"

"I worked with the man for ten fucking years! I need proof. I need to hear it from his own fucking mouth."

A warning creeps into his voice. "I mean it, Jack."

Blackness eats at my insides as we drive to Montreal, and I stare at the screen of my phone, filled with an ever-increasing mountain of dread.

She's not answering my texts.

My heart seizes. "She's not replying back."

"There's no way Sal could've realized we're on to him."

Doubt hangs on his words like sickly syrup.

"Can't this fucking car go any faster?"

My back slams into the car seat as he throttles the engine. "*Tabarnak de câlisse de criss de marde!*"

Johnny lets out a volley of curses as he grinds to a halt. I open the door and leap out of his car before it stops. A brief glimpse of the sign—a whale and a pitcher of beer—before I crash my shoulder into the door. It flies open and smashes into a group of people, and angry male voices rise up around me. My eyes scan the packed bar, but I don't see my wife's blonde head anywhere.

"Is she here?"

Johnny joins me and I say nothing as I walk toward the back. The dread is like a wildfire, burning back logic.

Please, please let her be here.

But I know she won't be as I palm the door, hearing a small sucking noise as the door unsticks from the jamb. Nothing prepares me for the way my lungs crush at the sight of the empty room.

"NO!"

My hands grip the edge of the table, where there's a single pad of notebook paper and a pencil, and I flip the fucking thing over. It makes a huge noise, the aluminum crashing loudly into the cement floor. Where the *fuck* is she? Where did he take her?

"*Shit.*"

Johnny's shoes clip over the stone as he walks in and his eyes scan the place.

"How the fuck did he know we were on to him?"

I don't know and I don't give a shit.

My vision blurs as I walk back into the bar, scanning the crowd of heads for her and finding nothing. Blood churning, I walk toward the bar and lunge at the bartender steadily wiping a glass.

"What the fuck?"

Grabbing his arms, I lift him over the bar and slam his face into the counter. "*Where the fuck is my wife*?"

"Ow! What the hell, man!"

"Answer the fucking question."

A set of furious blue eyes look at me under my palm as I grind his face into the counter. "I don't know!"

He does.

"You know who the hell I am. Don't get cute with me, or I'll take you out back and you'll have a real fucking problem."

I seize his arm and twist it behind his back, applying enough pressure to make him scream.

"She left with that fat guy!"

"Who?"

"Sal!"

"Did they say where they were going?"

The eyes narrow with incredulity. "Of course not. Please, let me go!"

Fuck.

What the hell is he doing? Why Beatrice? Killing my brother wasn't enough. He had to stab me in the heart just when I was finally getting my life together. He could be anywhere doing anything to her.

I loosen my grip on the bartender's head, and the room spins slightly.

I can't lose her.

I *love* her.

My lungs tighten so that I feel like I'm breathing through a straw—images of my brother's body and Beatrice's smiling face strike me like blows to my stomach. I crumple in on myself and gasp a desperate breath. A strong hand slides over my shoulder and anchors over my muscle, squeezing hard.

"Jack, we'll find her."

I just don't know.

"I swear to Christ, we'll find her."

What sort of state will she be in when we do?

BEATRICE

Waiting sucks.

I've never been a big fan. Doctor appointments, hair salons, really anywhere you're required to wait, I always loathed. Which is why I'm usually glued to my smart phone in these situations to pass the time.

But I'd give anything right now—slit my wrists, donate a kidney—to know Jack's all right. I can't bide my time playing a goddamn game. My husband's out there, doing something insanely stupid. Kill a boss? You don't kill bosses or presidents lightly. There are consequences. Debts.

We should have just left town.

I stand up from the long table as Sal's eyes follow me. There's strain written all over his face. His shoulders roll forward and he seems boxed in. Tense. It does little to soothe my nerves.

Jack's out there, *alone*. And he's just sitting there!

"Sal, why haven't you called anyone? Jack might need help."

He shifts his bulk, his eyes flicking away from me. "What am I supposed to do, lead a fucking coup against our boss? I'll be shot for suggesting it."

"*Don't act like this was his idea.*"

"It was his idea."

"You already betrayed your boss. *Here*. When you let Jack leave without a fight."

A nasty smile stretches across his face. "You're a pretty ballsy woman to talk to me like that."

Oh please. What are you going to do, hit me?

I have to keep reminding myself that these Mafia assholes have an ego the size of Quebec.

"He needs help."

Sal's eyes slide to mine. The look he throws me sends a spear through me.

"Sit down and shut up."

My fists ball at the table as heat rises to my cheeks. Weakening, my knees buckle.

He's not allowed to talk to you like that.

Jack's raw voice, unbidden, speaks in my ear as if he stands right beside me.

What am I supposed to do?

Kick his fucking ass.

The voice and its laughter fade in my ear as courage quails. What the hell am I supposed to do? What can I do? Jack might not be able to handle this on his own, and if he can't? Well, then my baby grows up without a father.

A cold shudder runs through my body. *No.*

Jesus, what about Maya? That son of a bitch is her husband—I completely forgot! Shit.

I stand back up and move around the table, heading for the door. One of the goons stationed at the door blocks my exit with his body.

"Get out of my way!"

"Your husband wants you to stay put."

"*Shut up, both of you*!"

A merry tune fills the small room as Sal digs his hand into his trousers and pulls out his phone.

Oh my God.

I hold my breath.

"Sal," he answers in a clipped voice. "Yeah, she's still here. What happened? Shit. *Jesus.* Yeah, we're on our way!"

"What happened?"

Sal ends the call laboriously and pitying eyes focus on me. "Looks like Jack got into a car accident before he could get to John's house."

My voice goes up at least one octave. "What?"

"He's hurt pretty bad. We need to get to the hospital *now.*"

Jack's hurt, and this time it's not just a sprained arm or a broken wrist. It's serious. A sob catches in my throat.

My wavering voice screams at the men. "Well, let's go!"

He nods to them and they step aside, letting me through the bar. Sal is close behind, huffing slightly as he keeps pace with me. I sprint outside, imagining a twisted wreck of smoking metal and mangled limbs. Oh God.

"How bad is it?" I ask him, close to tears. "Did they say?"

"They didn't want to talk about it on the phone."

"Where's your car?"

"This way."

I follow him to the Saturn parked out front. One of his goons opens the door for me and I slide in, twisting my hand in my lap.

Keep it together. He's fine. He's Jack—practically indestructible.

My eyes start to sting. He's hurt pretty bad, that's what Sal said.

The car starts and I throttle back in my seat. Wheezing from the blow to my back, I think about the pain he must be in right now. My mind races, trying to find the last time I felt his lips on my skin. I think about the way my body sang when he pulled me over his lap that first time I saw him, and then I hate myself for this macabre replay of our relationship.

Have some fucking faith that I'm all right.

Buildings whisk by the window as we drive up the ramp to the highway.

"Which hospital is he at?"

"Some place northeast."

I nod, hardly listening to his response. Then something jumps from the back of my brain and my heart starts pounding as if I snorted a line of coke.

"Wait—doesn't Johnny live downtown?"

"Yeah."

So why the fuck are we going the wrong way?

The silence pricks my skin like needles. "Where are we going?"

"I told you—the hospital."

"Yeah, but—"

"Shut the fuck up!"

Something is *really* wrong. Sal wipes his sweaty face with a huge hand as he drives, and the two guys behind him—my heart clenches painfully. They're cleaning their guns.

"Where are you taking me? *Where's Jack*?"

Sal's voice is too calm. "Relax, we're taking you to him."

Forced calm washes over me, but the scenery outside makes my hackles rise again.

"Cut the bullshit—where's Jack?"

A few seconds pass before Sal speaks again. "Out killing Johnny, I hope."

"He's not in an accident?"

Relief floods my veins when he shakes his head. The soothing wave evaporates when I realize he fucking tricked me.

"Fuck, biker sluts must be dumb," chimes a voice in the back. "You don't catch on quick, do you?"

Fear pounds its way through my veins.

"Then what the hell are you doing with me—where are we going?"

"To end this fucking thing."

My blood runs cold at the sound of that. End this thing? My hands grapple the door, but we're on the goddamn highway. I can't just jump out—plus, the baby.

"Your fucking funeral," Sal says with a laugh.

A voice interrupts from the back. "Boss, what the fuck are we doing?"

He looks into his rearview mirror to address the man behind me. "Change of plans—"

"What? You said we just had to wait for Jack to take care of Johnny."

Shock reverberates inside my ribs. What's going on?

"I don't think he's going to go through with it. He *might*."

My phone rings in my lap and I try to stifle the noise, but Sal leans over and crushes my hand in his. Joints pop as he twists the phone and wrenches it free, and then he looks at the screen. It's Jack. He's calling me.

"He didn't do it. *God fucking dammit*!"

His meaty fist smashes into the dashboard and the car swerves, almost hitting the median. My scream hits the air, piercing our ears.

"SHUT THE FUCK UP OR I'LL BLOW YOUR HEAD OFF!"

My voice trembles into a quiet gasp as he slips the gun out of his coat and aims it at my face.

"You are going to fucking help me kill John, or you're dead."

I raise my hands, heart pounding so loud that I'm sure the whole car can hear it. "I—I can't—"

"Put your fucking hands down, now."

Gripping the steering wheel, he tucks his gun back into his jacket as I lower my arms.

"Just shut the fuck up and don't make a scene."

"This is fucking serious. If Jack didn't do it then we're fucked."

Sal twists his head around to glare at them. "You think I didn't have another fucking plan in case the asshole changed his mind? Jesus."

"What is it?"

His slippery smile is directed toward me. "We use her."

* * *

The winding road spirals up the hill, twisting around a forest of pines. My heart jackknifes in my chest when I realize where we are. The compound. *Home*. My parents.

The place that shunned me.

The place that's going to bury me.

Why the hell is he taking me here?

The car door's metallic lock shines in the sunlight. All I have to do is wait for them to slow down enough during a bend in the road and open the door.

I'm not going to fucking walk in there like an animal led to slaughter.

"I'm not going to help kill Maya's husband, so you might as well kill me now."

Sal turns his head and smiles at me. "I think you'll change your tune soon enough."

Fuck him.

I throw my body against the door as I turn the handle just as the car slows down enough for me to jump out. The roar of the engine hits my ears as I bail, the earth slamming into my side and knocking the air from my body.

"Fuck!"

A screech of car tires—the sound of pairs of feet, moving rapidly.

Get up!

The world spins as I roll down a ditch. My back slams against the trunk of a tall pine and needles cascade down my face. For a second I sit there, stunned that I just jumped out of a moving car. Then footsteps crash through the brush.

I shoot up like a rabbit and fly into the dark woods. Tree branches whip me as I hurtle through the forest, desperate to get away.

Where the fuck am I going?

I've no phone—no way to contact Jack and tell him where I am.

"Come back, you bitch!"

Sal's labored breathing wheezes behind me and I dart away from him, but then a blur collides with my body and we crash heavily to the ground. I cry out in pain as one of the men lifts off me and grabs my hair, forcing me to kneel.

I stare into the endless black tunnel, and I wonder how a perfect, dark circle could bring me so much dread. The thumb moves up, cocking the gun. The metallic sound freezes my blood.

Oh God, I don't want to die.

One of these days, you're going to have to stand up for yourself.

Jack's powerful voice booms in my ear, and my chest swells. He's right.

"Ready to die, princess?"

With great effort I tear my eyes from the muzzle and stare at Sal's impassive face. "You're not going to kill me. You *need* me."

"Listen, maybe we should get rid of the bitch and bring her body there. We could tell the MC Johnny sent his guys after her and get them on our side."

"That's a stupid idea!" I flinch as he digs the gun into my forehead.

"Oh yeah? Why's that?" he sneers.

"The MC doesn't give a shit about me."

He makes a shrugging motion. "Fair point."

"She'll say whatever the fuck she wants to save her ass!"

"I'm not going to waste the only hostage I have. Get her up. Let's go."

Rough hands seize under my arms and haul me upright as despair hits my chest like a mallet.

I'm sorry, Jack. I tried!

"How the hell are we going to get into the compound without them filling us with lead?"

A smirk creeps into Sal's voice. "I've been in talks with the vice president for some time. He's not happy with Jett. Bending over backward to appease the family made him a lot of enemies. I told him if he helped me get rid of John, I'd help him whack Jett."

The vice president? I try to dig up what I know about Reg, the lean biker with a midnight-black, stubbly beard, streaks of gray peppering his dark head. He's one of the guys who came into power after Maya's father was killed.

"And then what? You think they're just going to let you skip out of there unharmed?"

"Once I'm boss, I'll cut the MC a better deal. Something that's way more fair. They'd be fucking stupid to refuse me."

Shit!

A broad hand shoves my back and we stumble blindly back to the car. My brain whirs wildly, trying to think. Think! Nothing. My mind draws up a blank space of white.

Sal's round face looks back at me. "Jesus, will you relax? You'll be fine. Johnny is the only one I want."

He's lying, Jack's voice whispers in my ear. *He's fucking lying. Fight!*

Do something!

I can't do a damn thing with a gun at my back.

Bide your time. There'll be an opportunity. Don't freeze up.

I won't, I tell the voice. *I won't.*

JACK

"Where the *fuck* is she?"

A scrawny man writhes in my grip like a cat until I slam his back against the brick wall. "I've *no* idea who you're talking about!"

"My WIFE!"

His head hits the wall with a dull thud and his hands fall from my wrist. A flash of irritation sears my body as his knees buckle and he drops to the street. He lies there, oddly still. I nudge him with my foot. Nothing.

Fuck.

"Jack, what the hell are you doing?"

Johnny peers in the alley, his eyes widening at the man crumpled at my feet.

"*Maudit*, Jack!" His hand wraps around my throat as he shoves me against the wall, snarling in my face. "I know you're worried about your wife, but that does not mean you get to act like a fucking idiot."

"I'm losing my *fucking* mind! Where the hell did he take her?"

He gives me one last shove and steps back from me, agitated. "I don't know. I have no fucking clue what he's thinking."

The unspoken question burns my eyes. *Do you think she's dead?*

No, damn it. I can't let my mind linger on that for one second. If she's gone, I'm not a father or a husband anymore. I'm nothing but another soldier on the street.

And I can't go back to that.

"Come on."

He grips my arm and steers me to the door, rapping his knuckles on the metal frame. It opens, revealing the back room of *Le Zinc*. It's filled with only a few of Johnny's most trusted members, but I swallow a line of nausea as I look at them.

"Just have a seat and try not to fucking kill anyone."

I slump down in a chair as voices scream in my head—mostly her voice, filled with pain. My throat constricts and I check my phone again as a wave of anguish pours over me. Nothing there either.

Hushed voices surround me as they talk in somber tones. It's like I'm on my fucking deathbed—or at my brother's funeral. There's too much shit going on at once. We're at war with the Devils, and Sal conspired against the boss and took my wife. The family is fractured.

She's out there with that psychopath and I have no idea where she is.

Shaking, I stand up from my seat and check my phone for the millionth time, willing myself to not crack the screen in my firm grip. Sal's round, smiling rat face hovers in my vision, taunting me. I told her John was the devil, but *he* was. He killed Mike. Why? I just want to fucking hear it—I want him to fucking admit it through those foul lips.

"Take my wife and kid and get them the fuck out of the city." John's voice booms out of nowhere, and I look back as he talks to the New Yorker. "Don't let them out of your sight, Tommy. I'm trusting you with my family. Don't let me down."

"I won't."

Tommy shoots me a sympathetic look before walking out of the place. His footsteps echo sharply in the small room before the door shuts behind him. John runs a hand through his hair, looking shaken.

"Where the *fuck* is Sal! I've got the whole town in my pocket and no one knows where he is?"

I stand up suddenly as a jolt of electricity runs through me.

"What are you doing?"

"I can't just fucking sit here, John. I have to do *something.*"

A placating hand held toward me only strokes the flames of rage.

"I hear you."

No, you fucking don't!

Then my phone rings, cutting across the room. It's Beatrice's number. I almost drop the phone in shock.

"Everyone shut the fuck up!"

Trembling, I accept the call and hold the hot metal to my ear. A feminine voice breathes through the speaker. My heart tightens and releases.

"Hon, is that you?"

"*Jack*!"

"Where the hell are you? Are you hurt?"

Cold wraps around my guts like a fist as a deep male voice replaces hers. "Not yet."

Johnny leans forward, excitement widening his eyes.

I want to scream at that cool, detached voice. *Fuck you. Fuck your mother's rat-infested twat. I'm going to find you and rip you apart.*

"What are you doing, Sal?"

"Getting what I want."

The chair knocks to the floor and suddenly I'm standing upright, blood pounding in my ears. "Don't you fucking dare!"

"I want Johnny dead. If he's still alive, bring him to the MC compound, and I'll give back your little biker bitch."

Rage. I've never been this pissed in my life, never felt my brain squeezed like this, as though it were in a vise. "After Johnny's dead, then what? You become boss? Are you a fucking lunatic?"

"They can fall in line or die. I don't give a shit. Be here in three hours, or your wife's pretty brains will decorate this wall."

A stream of curses runs from my mouth, reverberating in my head like a stereo implanted in my brain. I don't even hear him hang up, just the roar of everything else.

A hand grasps my shoulder and arm, shaking me.

"What'd he say? Jack!"

It's as though there's a parasite lodged in my heart, sapping energy while growing with a poisonous throb. It hurts. I've never hurt this fucking bad in my life, even when Mike died.

Even if I could, I'd never walk out of there breathing. That's a fucking fact.

John grabs the back of my neck, squeezing hard. "Tell me."

"He's at the MC."

"Which MC? Goddamn it, Jack—"

"The Devils. He wants me to bring you there. He wants you dead."

The room breaks with that last sentence, the tension snapped like a guitar string.

"We should have never trusted those biker pieces of shit!"

I keep speaking in a monotone voice. "I have a few hours to bring him John, or he'll kill my wife."

That last sentence hangs in the air like an obscene phrase. It's too horrible to contemplate. Biker daughter or not, she's still my wife. A fellow wise guy going after his brother's wife? There are lines that are never crossed in the life. Sal took a piss on that line and lit it on fire. He's trashing everything we believe in. No fucking way will anyone willingly work for him.

"So that's how he wants to play?" Johnny's eyes are overwrought as menace creeps into his voice. "That goddamn moron won't know what hit him."

"That place is surrounded by reinforced concrete, John. How the fuck are we getting in there?"

"By giving him what he wants. Me."

What?

A manic grin stretches Johnny's face. "And maybe a peace offering."

Other voices chime in with ideas, and my heart pounds harder when I realize what Johnny means to do.

"Sal's mine," I tell the room of people. "Touch him and you'll have to answer to me."

And when I get ahold of him, there'll be no mercy.

* * *

Johnny's heavy weight slumps over my shoulder as I carry him in a fireman's lift. The floodlights of the compound bathe us in light. I let his body tumble from my arms to hit the ground hard, and he lets out a painful wheeze, rolling on his back. His gasps fill the night sky as the light washes over his wounds. I had to knock him around a few times to make him look fucked up. I won't say that a part of me didn't enjoy it a little.

His hands are bound behind his back with a zip tie, carefully filed down so that a bit of pressure will release him.

God, I hope this works.

A man appears on the battlements of the fortress. Someone I don't recognize.

"You brought him." His smooth voice holds an inflection of surprise.

"Where is Sal?"

I'm aware of the automatic guns trained on my chest right now.

"He's inside with your wife."

I can't wait until I can wipe that smile from your face.

I can't fight the tremble in my voice. "I want to see her."

A frown tightens his face. "She should have never been given to you. You didn't deserve her."

I bristle as the door rolls open only wide enough to admit a stream of bikers outside. They surround me, ignoring the truck I arrived in. Two of them pick up Johnny's body and drag him across the dirt. A fierce poke to my back prompts me forward.

A small crowd of bikers stands in the courtyard, their postures menacing. They frisk me and take my concealed guns. I feel the loss with a small twinge of anger. Johnny's sprawled body lies in the dirt and I see the biker who spoke to me slowly descending the staircase from the wall.

"Where the fuck is the president?"

"My name is Reg. I'm president now."

Fuckhead.

The cocky asshole stops a foot in front of me and then recognition slowly worms into my mind. He was the VP—a guy I barely knew.

"Where's Jett?"

He points to a distance about fifty meters away, to a huddled mass curled on the ground. Blood stains his leather cut. It looks like there's a hole blown right in the middle of it. Jesus.

"He deserved to die the moment he handed over one of our own like a common whore."

My insides knot. "Where's my fucking wife?"

An impish smile creeps over his lips. "Why should I give her back to you?"

"Maybe you'll find out why after I shove my fist up your ass."

A gun slams into my back, the dull pain cracking over my bones as Reg laughs his ass off.

"Relax. We owe our friend here a great debt for bringing us the Cravotta boss."

He jerks his head and the doors of the clubhouse open. A slim, blonde woman stumbles out and a huge weight lifts from my shoulders. Beatrice. She's okay.

Her hair spills over her shoulders like liquid gold and I hear her delicate cries from across the courtyard. My senses flame into overdrive.

"Jack!"

Hearing the desperate cry from her lips feels like a hand reaching between my ribs and yanking. I stride forward to bring her into my arms, to soothe that ache in my chest.

An arm catches me.

"Whoa," Reg says. "Slow down. We're not done here."

I'd like to take the arm stopping me from holding my wife and rip it off.

"What are you talking about?"

He cocks his head. "What's with the truck?"

Truck? Jesus, I almost forgot.

"It's a peace offering. That thing is stacked with the arms we were going to sell to the MC."

Reg eyes me like a shark. "Let me get this straight. I help Sal hide your woman from you, and you give me a gift?"

His boots scrape at the dirt as he prowls around Johnny's limp body. A motion with his hand makes them prop him up to a sitting position. His head lolls on his shoulder and Reg's palm slaps him. Johnny's eyes open dramatically.

"Do you take me for a fucking idiot? Let me guess, it's loaded with your men or a bomb."

"Wrong," I say, fighting to keep my voice even. "Send out your men to check it if you think I'm lying."

"It has to be rigged to blow."

A growl rumbles my chest. "If you think I'd risk my wife's life like that, you're a fucking moron."

He yanks the gun from his side and grabs the scruff of my neck, burying the muzzle in my flesh. Beatrice cries out, and then I see Sal behind her, yanking her back.

Take your fucking hands off her.

His breath billows over my cheeks. "You're pretty fucking brave to call me a moron."

Don't fuck this up, Jack.

"There's nothing in there that'll hurt anyone in this MC."

That, at least, was perfectly true. I force myself not to make eye contact with Johnny. Fuck, we have to speed this up.

Reg's dark eyes scan me, and he smiles. "Go," he says to the bikers clustered at the gate. "Search it. Check for false walls—everything."

A few tense minutes pass in the courtyard, and my eyes find Beatrice, who stands just within reach of the man responsible for making my life a living hell. The plan runs through my mind, but I don't give a fuck about killing bikers.

I just want her.

"Prez!" one of them shouts, minutes later. "Everything looks good. Tons of ammunition in there."

Reg's smile widens. "Well, well, well. Drive it in."

Yes.

The headlights of the truck illuminate the packed earth, casting deep shadows over its grooves. The engine growls and the wheels crack the ground. The head of the truck passes the gate. Then with a loud whine and a violent shudder, the engine stalls. It stops.

This is it.

"What the fuck happened?" Confused, Reg takes a step forward and Johnny's eyes open, wide and alert. His hands twist behind his back. They break free of the zip tie.

A speeding black mass howls toward the fortress, and the loud roar confuses them.

"What the fuck did you do?"

He whirls around as the car smashes through the gate, past the stalled truck. Another one follows it, and muzzles flash like fireworks in the dark. I hurl myself to the ground as Johnny slips the blade from his sleeve and slashes at the heels of the man standing behind him. The bikers fire back at the two cars, windows exploding. I help John tackle the man and we wrestle the gun from his hand. Pop-pop. Two gunshots to his temple silence him immediately. I seize the gun strapped to his ankle, and bullets pepper the ground next to me. Where's Beatrice?

She's gone, disappeared in the chaos. Probably with that rat, Sal. Fuck.

The guys in the cars are pinned. Blood streaks down into little puddles. I grit my teeth as screams erupt around me and sprint around the clubhouse for cover. I grab the back of Johnny's jacket and yank him around the corner.

"This is fucking crazy."

Behind Johnny's back, there's movement. I raise my hand and fire, and a biker drops his gun, dead.

Johnny claps my shoulder in thanks.

"I need to find her."

A stream of men pours out of the clubhouse, and for a moment it looks like it's going to be a slaughter. They aim their guns, firing at the backs of their own brothers.

"What the fuck?"

A wry grin crawls over John's face. "Sal's not the only one with deep ties to the MC. Let's go find your wife."

I flatten myself against the wall and use the butt of my pistol to smash a window. The glass sticks out in jagged pieces and I climb carefully into a darkened bedroom. Thank God it's empty. Johnny climbs in after me and lands with a soft thump. Our footsteps creak on the floorboards.

"We just have to check room by room. He's here somewhere."

My hand finds the doorknob in the dark and I twist it open. I burst out, turning left as I aim my gun down the hallway. Johnny turns to the right.

"Clear."

We inch down the hall, kicking open another door that holds a group of frightened children. One look at their tearstained faces brings a swell of rage for the MC. I slam the door shut, knowing that it's a matter of time before we'll open a door and someone will be ready for us.

Heart rate jacked, I palm open a door and feel a rush of air. A scream of pain explodes in my ear and I fire into the direction of the sounds. A biker holding a rifle slumps over on the upturned bucket and crashes to the ground.

"Fuck!"

Shit. Johnny!

He clutches his shoulder, eyes screwed up in pain as the hand holding his gun falls limp at his side.

"Shot."

"Fuck!"

No, no, no!

I throw Johnny's arm over my shoulder and drag him to the closest empty room, depositing him on a bed. His suit is wet with blood and a trickle of red pours out of his sleeve.

"Fucking bastard got me."

I grab the sheets from the bed and tear at them with my knife.

"It'll be all right. Looks like it went right through."

"*Putain.*" He hisses in pain as I peel away his suit and knife away his shirt. A dark hole floods with blood in the meat of his shoulder. I look around his back and see the exit wound.

"My wife's going to fucking kill me."

The mention of his wife reminds me of mine, still lost—still in the grasp of that psycho. I wrap the sheet around his shoulder, looping it under his arm and tying a tight knot so that he winces in pain.

"Okay. Stay here."

"Fuck that," he growls. "I'm not going to just sit here."

"Boss, you're hurt. Stay put. We can't survive if you die."

He stands up, his color dulled. Something more than pain swirls in his eyes. "I never wanted Mike dead. I would never do that to one of my own."

It's the closest I'll ever get to, "I'm sorry."

"I know. I'm sorry I didn't believe you."

I turn away from him and open the door, getting one last look of him sitting down on the mattress, giving me a stiff nod. Then I close it behind me and I run into a thick body. We collide, and my gun flies from my hand. Then I notice that black-bearded face—that fucking asshole who taunted me in the courtyard. Reg.

I tackle him before he can recover, his back slamming into the wall. His knee hits my guts and I let go, winded. Then a sharp elbow strikes my back and I'm knocked down. My body sprawls as pain radiates from both sides, then I lunge for my handgun. It scrapes on the wood. Reg's legs straddle me, and then I twist around. BAM!

Black pools widen with shock as his huge hands clutch his stomach.

I pick myself up, enjoying the sight of the biker writhing on the floor, hand on his bleeding guts.

"What the fuck did you say to me? I didn't deserve Beatrice?"

He mouths something incoherent.

"Fuck you."

I kick his hands away from his stomach and I press down on his gunshot wound with my foot. Screams tear through the distant rat-tat-at of gunfire outside.

I would kill him, but I need to save every round for Sal.

Blood spurts from his mouth, and then I know he isn't long for this world anyway. Better to let the fucking prick die a slow death.

I step over his body, eyes scanning the deserted club. Where the fuck is he? I look through windows, and then I see shadows in the president's office. Vito and Tim stand outside as sentries.

Bingo.

They're Sal's men.

I suck in breath as I raise my gun, visualizing the attack in my head. Two shots in quick succession. My chest deflates as I exhale. Shots ring out in the clubhouse—too fast for them to react. They slump down dead as red paints the walls behind them.

I make a beeline for the door and wipe my palms on my slacks, sucking in air. Aim and fire. Do it quickly. Don't hesitate. She's too important.

I kick open the door, and her scream sends a frenzy through my system. Beatrice is thrust in front of me, that fat fuck hiding behind her like a coward.

"I'll fucking kill her. Not another step."

He grabs her hair like a ponytail and yanks her backward so that she sits on his lap, his pistol buried in her neck.

"Jack!"

Christ, I can't bear the sound of her crying, so I force myself to look into that rat bastard's eyes.

My gun hovers, trembling. "Why?"

For years I depended on him. Trusted him. He was like a second father to me—a guy who always had my back. Why would he betray everything he had built with me?

"Why what?"

"Why did you kill him? He was my brother. Everyone loved him."

Sal looks back at me, his face infused with rage. "I needed to create a reason for you to hate Johnny. It was nothing personal."

Nothing personal.

There's nothing but detachment in his voice. Just business. No big deal.

I almost fire a bullet into his fucking brain right then. "You ruined my life."

"Jack, what the fuck was I supposed to do? Your brother was paralyzed—he didn't even want to live. The guys who did it said he didn't even struggle—"

"DON'T LIE TO ME!"

His round face wrinkles as he adopts a stricken tone. "I needed Johnny to go. Look at what he's done to this family. He made peace with these fucking savages after what they did to your brother. He's weak."

I'm still putting it together, seething with rage. I have to find out every detail. I need to know the depths of his treachery.

"You tried to have me killed at that arms deal, didn't you?" I recall how they aimed at me and fired.

"They weren't supposed to touch you. I just wanted to start a war to pull John in different directions."

A vicious hatred churns in my guts. "Then you had them come after my wife."

He shrugs remorselessly. "I needed to give your ass a kick to go after John."

And it worked.

"You are one sick son of a bitch. When I get my hands on you—"

Beatrice cries out as he digs the metal into her flesh. "Put the gun down. I'll pull the trigger *right now*. There's nothing stopping me."

"It's over. You lost."

For the first time, Sal looks angry. His face burns a deep red. "Not yet!"

"I just put a bullet in the new president's stomach."

"Miserable cocksucker!" He grips her neck and she makes a sputtering sound. "Have you any fucking idea what I would have done for the family? You would've been promoted—I was going to make you underboss!"

"Like I give a fuck about being your lapdog. You're just a fucking snake, too cowardly to get rid of John yourself."

Beatrice's hands roll something in the waistband of her jeans, and I see a glint of silver.

No, don't!

Her blue eyes blaze at me.

"Put the fucking gun down!"

I splay my hands, lowering my body slowly as I let the gun dangle in my hand.

She screams, and Sal adjusts his grip on her neck to muffle the sound, but she twists in his arms.

"AH!"

The gun slips from her neck as she buries the switchblade in his belly. Bright red spills over her hand as she pulls out the knife and stabs him again and again. Shock paralyzes me for a moment.

Then I lunge at the arm holding the gun and it fires. The bullet lodges into a picture frame. Even though Sal's got a fucking knife sticking out of his stomach, he's still strong. Heavy blows smash across my jaw, but I dig my thumbs into his eyes until he screams. Beatrice holds my gun, aiming at him. I grab her skinny wrist and aim at his head.

"FUCK!"

One pull of the trigger cracks open Sal's head. A dark-red stain paints the wall as he slides down to our feet, dead.

Jesus Christ.

Beatrice makes a whimpering sound, and I'm still worked up into a frenzy. It's still not real.

"What the fuck were you thinking?" I scream at her pale face. "You almost got killed!"

"I had to do something," she says, looking at her bright-red hands in shock. "I couldn't just sit there."

Her smooth skin glides under my hands as I take her head, my chest ballooning with gratefulness. "What would I have done without you?"

If she died because of me, I don't think there would ever be any getting out of the hole I'd fall into.

Those rosebud lips tremble. "I love you."

I bend my face, forgetting that there's a fucking war outside. I need to soothe the horrifying ache in my chest. She almost died. The woman I love almost lost her life and our baby's life.

I barely touch her, the relief pouring into me so painful that I have to bite my lip to keep from crying out. I inhale deeply, steeling myself as I thread my hand through her gorgeous hair. She gasps as I yank hard. "Never, ever do that again."

I want to take her right now—teach her a goddamn lesson. I know it's fucking crazy, but my dick jumps at the thought of taking her in this club.

A tear slides down her face. "I'm sorry."

The sadness choking her throat makes me break, and I pull her into my arms, certain that I'll never let go of her.

* * *

The fog from the shower clouds the glass, but I watch the shadow of her figure move like an erotic private show. Even when my body is scored with cuts and bruises and I feel like collapsing over my bed, fucking my wife still consumes my thoughts. My hand strays to my cock, which grows uncomfortably hard beneath my briefs. I slide them off and pull off my shirt, and then I step to the shower door and grasp the handle.

Steam rolls out of the shower as I open the door, revealing Beatrice's wet, naked curves. My cock makes an impatient twitch and I join her. Her blonde hair darkens under the water, making her skin glow as she stands under the hot stream. Her lips pull into a small, tired smile. Small hands reach around my waist and pull me against her. I hold her as my heart tightens and releases in a way I've never felt before.

She soaps my back and I let her wash me. Her hands curl around my balls and glide up my shaft. My cock hardens under her grip and she gives me a sly grin.

"We need to talk about what happened."

The smile playing on her face falters. "What about it?"

You risked your life.

My hands slide from the curve of her back to the gentle slope of her stomach and those beautiful tits. I seize her nipples and pinch hard.

"You said you would listen to every word I said. You didn't listen. You were fucking reckless."

Beatrice flinches at my tone. "What was I supposed to do, just let him kill you?"

"It wouldn't have gone down like that. We're having a baby," I growl, my nails biting into her nipples. She exhales a sigh that makes my dick throb as my hands caress her tits, moving back down under her ass to lift her in my arms. I brace her back against the glass.

"You can't risk that life inside you for anything. Do you fucking understand?"

She glares at me steadily.

No, she doesn't.

I catch her bottom lip between my teeth and I bite down. Then I move my iron-stiff cock right between her legs, rubbing her clit. She moans in between kissing me back.

"Your job is to raise my kids. Mine is to provide and keep you safe."

"I—I know."

The length of me slides along her pussy and ecstasy hits me like a live wire. Fuck, I'll always need her pussy. Over her shoulder I catch a glimpse of that smoking-hot tattoo. *Property of Jack.*

"You know damn well." My hand rips over her ass, blood rushing to her skin as the sound cracks the air.

"Why can't you be sweet with me?" she says with a sigh.

My heart wants to. I want to carry her in my arms and lay her down on my bed. I want to make love to her, and not fuck her hard like I need to.

"I can't give you what you want when you don't behave."

My lips crush against hers in a long, deep kiss. Her eyes dance when I pull back, her chest burning red.

"I love you."

She keeps saying that as her defense. It pulls at my heart and pisses me off at the same time. I love her, too. That's why I need to show her who's boss.

Her eyes widen when I push my hips, the head of my cock spreading her open slightly. "Remember the rules?"

"Yes."

"You're not going to come until I want you to."

A bit of pressure opens up her pussy, the lips guiding my cock inside as a moan shudders through the stream of water. It's incredibly hot to see myself buried balls deep. The marks I made earlier today shine in angry red blotches all over her tits.

I keep my dick anchored inside her as I grind her. Her heart beats against my chest as I crush her body, kissing her neck.

"There's another part of your job I forgot to mention. Can you guess what it is?"

Beatrice utters an incomprehensible moan.

"It's to spread those beautiful legs for your husband, whenever he wants." I pull back, watching as the vein on my cock throbs.

"Your job is to take my cock and milk me dry."

She cries out as I slowly sink back inside her. Her lips seek me out, but I hold her head straight. I want her desperate. My tongue runs over her neck and I bite down. She gasps at the sudden sting and then sighs in relief when I wet her with my tongue.

"Yes, I want it!"

I really lucked out getting such a horny wife. Then I reach down and massage that swollen clit, pinching it tight as her slick walls clench my dick, wanting more of me. I slide out, even though it's torture.

"I know you do," I say in a chuckle, ramming her hard again. "I'm not going to stop coming inside that sweet cunt until I have enough kids to satisfy me."

And even then it'll be hard not to fuck her bareback, to feel her raw pussy gripping my cock. Goddamn, it makes me so fucking worked up to think that I knocked her up. All those nights in Vegas when we were trying to have a baby. She wanted it so fucking badly that she'd cry when the tests were negative. Every goddamn day she was begging for my cum. It was some of the hottest sex I've ever had, and I want it again. I want it over and over. And I want a family—a big family.

Even though I know she's pregnant, the urge to fill her up consumes me like a fire, eating away at my flesh. I need her. I need this fucking hot body to be mine.

My balls slap against her wetly as I pound her against the glass. The water washes away some of the lubrication, and it hurts, but it also feels really damn good. Especially when she claws my shoulders.

"Jack! Can I come? Please?"

I slow down and pull out of her, even though I want to drive right back in.

"No."

Then I let her down, my cock screaming for release. I kneel at her feet and spread her legs apart. With my head right under her pussy, I use my thumbs to spread her lips apart and then I stroke that jeweled nub with my tongue.

"Jack! Oh God!"

I reach back and lick her silky pussy as water heats my body. Her taste fills my mouth and I drink greedily like a man starved of thirst. I close my mouth around her and suck, feeling her muscles quivering around my tongue. It buries inside her until my nose smashes her cunt, and then I pull back, flicking her clit.

"Oh Jesus, Jack!"

Man, it turns me on to hear her scream my name. It rebounds sharply off the tiles, as well as the swift slap across her ass.

I spread her apart again, loving how flushed she is and the way she digs her fingers into my hair, trying to yank me upright. Instead my finger slides into her soaking pussy and she grinds against me. I pull it out and curl my tongue in her wetness. She yanks hard.

"Fuck me, Jack."

I ignore her.

"I'm sorry for—for what I did, just please!"

I stand up before she can get the last words out. "I don't believe you."

Her wet lashes blink at me plaintively and I draw her in. She presses her lips against mine, hungrily seeking out my tongue.

"Do you like tasting yourself?"

"Yes."

Dirty girl.

She barely answers before crushing my lips again, her moans shuddering through my mouth.

"Please," she cries. "I swear I'll never do it again."

I hold her flushed face until she stills. "No one will ever hurt you again."

Then I grab her waist and spin her around, shoving her back down so that she plants both palms on the fogged glass. Her beautiful ass rises to me, the black calligraphy winking at me: *Property of Jack.* I grab a fistful of her ass and slap her. My palm stings with the force of the blow, and I watch as my handprint sears over her skin. My cock pounds with an ache, the head dripping as I pull her cheeks apart and dive into her warmth. She throws her golden head back and buckles against my thrusts. My eyes devour every inch of her body. There's not a part of her that I don't like. Everything, from the shape of her pink nipples to the mound of her pussy, to the way her ass jiggles when I fuck her from behind. Her walls feel like smooth silk, tightening over my cock. They pull at me, and I dive back in. Her breath cuts off with every stroke. High cries hit the ceiling as I lean in, grabbing her swaying tits. I slap *Property of Jack*, loving her for getting that tattoo.

"I love you!"

Goddamn it.

I've heard it from other women before, of course, but it never gave me a thrill like it does now. Never wanted to say it back.

"Come, baby. Do it for me."

She lets out a whine and bucks against me. My balls slap her hard enough to hurt me and then I keep my dick lodged inside her. Convulsions ride like a wave along my cock, and she grinds me with a long moan that makes my dick pulse. Blonde hair twists around my hand as I pull her head, making her arch into that elegant slope. The need burns with hotter flames and it's so fucking hot in the shower. The blistering heat beats on my back, heightening every sensation until I feel drunk. I yank her, she bounces off my hips, and the pressure builds—then all of a sudden I feel the release.

It's pure gold. Ecstasy. Tension leaves my body as my cock swells inside her, claiming her body as mine. I feel the burst, the sweet release of pressure. Then her pussy feels warm and wet, and I keep digging my cock in, pushing my cum deep as I'm driven by instinct.

My cock twitches, the sensation gripping my thigh. Breathing hard, I reach back and dial down the heat. She stands up and lies against the glass wall with her forearms, completely exhausted. My arm curls around her waist and she turns, her freckles burning.

"I love you, too."

BEATRICE

"Walk to *Papa*!"

My cousin grips my baby's chubby hands for balance as he walks on shaky feet. Jack kneels on charcoal-gray slacks in the middle of Johnny's living room, his hands outstretched toward his son.

"Go on. Walk!"

Michael turns his head toward my voice and stumbles toward me. "Mama!"

A smile pulls at my lips as my baby boy's face wrinkles with a smile. "No, *papa*! Go to *papa*!"

"Come," Jack says in a stronger voice.

The one-year-old totters faster, Maya holding on to his hands until we cheer. Michael squeals with delight as his father takes him in his arms and kisses his cheek. A warm glow fills my chest when Jack cradles our son, a brilliant smile on his face.

"Mama!" A two-year-old boy with thick, dark-brown curls runs from Johnny's legs and tugs on his mother's skirt.

"What is it?"

His eyes glaze with tears as he looks at the baby receiving all the attention. Maya gives me a knowing grin.

"Aw, he's jealous. Come here, Matteo."

The shy toddler walks to me with urging from his mother, "Go to your *zia*," and I hoist him in my arms. He plays with my shirt and I smile at Johnny, who stands across the room. Only a year ago he wouldn't let me touch his son. Now he's godfather to Michael. My life feels like a dream. Every day I wake up, expecting them all to vanish, but I'm still just as happy as I was the day before.

"Let's go outside. Food's ready!"

Jack follows Johnny through the living room, but Maya stops for a second, her hand still over her swollen belly.

"What is it?"

"Just kicking."

Relief floods my cousin's face as we continue walking to the patio outside, where a charcoal grill hisses with sausage links and hamburgers. I watch them interact outside, marveling at the change between them. Ever since that night at the clubhouse, things have been different. Johnny warmed up to both of us and started inviting me over when everything cooled down.

Thinking about the MC sends a dart of pain in my heart. For months it's been like walking on pins and needles. The president, Reg, somehow survived and there was a violent reshuffling in the leadership of the mob. Traitors had to be dealt with. Jack doesn't tell me much about it. The first few months were the worst, when I was holed up in a safe house with Maya. Then there was the stress of the indictments for the Trudeau heist, and then finally the Mafia and the MC hammered out a truce to stop the CSIS investigation in its tracks. Again.

Who knows how long it'll last.

My parents. Cousins. They're still at the fortress. The place I used to call home is closed to me forever.

The sadness gripping me brightens when Matteo grabs a chunk of my hair and tugs sharply. The frown on his pudgy face makes me burst into laughter.

"All *right.* All right."

I hand off Matteo to his mother, who buckles him into the child seat around the patio table.

"Sausages need a couple more minutes," Johnny says.

Jack wanders the yard and finally stops at my side, sliding an arm around my waist as he plants a kiss on my cheek. "Did we make a beautiful kid, or what?"

Heat slowly rises up my spine when he squeezes me and I stare into Michael's deep-brown eyes. They're exactly the same shape as his father's.

"Babe, I invited your parents over for dinner next week."

"What?"

A mischievous grin spreads over his handsome face as he quickly looks behind him. "Johnny doesn't have to know."

Tears prick my eyes. "They're really coming?"

"Yeah. I figure it's about time I meet them."

A soaring feeling fills my chest. "I can't believe you'd do that for me."

"Of course I would. I love you."

His arm pulls me tight and suddenly the world shines a lot brighter. The warmth of the sun seeps into my skin until I can feel my mood lifting. I share one last look with the man who gave me everything, and then we lose ourselves in another kiss.

# # #

ABOUT THE AUTHOR

Vanessa Waltz loves to write romantic suspense novels. She lives in the Bay Area with two crazy cats and she loves mail from her fans: **waltzbooks@gmail.com.**

Made in the USA
San Bernardino, CA
05 February 2016